'Oh, gentlemen, I b[illegible]
do, the only way my baby [illegible]
Her voice rang with anguish and mounted to a climax with a sonorous entreaty: 'I appeal to you, I beseech you, if I can't work for you we'll . . .'

'Stop, Mlle Bernhardt,' Montigny cried. 'I will find you something.' But Sarah was wrapped up in her performance. She was about to collapse.

'The baby!' cried Sardou. 'You will drop the baby!'

Montigny rushed forward. In grabbing the endangered bundle he removed the swaddling clothes. Out jumped the monkey . . .

ALAN ARNOLD

Sarah

based on the screenplay for the
Reader's Digest film, 'The Incredible Sarah' starring
Glenda Jackson

Collins
FONTANA BOOKS

First published by Fontana Books 1976

Made and printed in Great Britain by
William Collins Sons and Co Ltd Glasgow

I want to acknowledge a debt to certain works which provided me with new information about the ordeal of Paris in 1870 and the decline of Napoleon III's regime – Robert Baldick's enthralling *The Siege of Paris* and S. C. Burchel's fascinating *The Upstart Empire* – and to J. B. Priestley's *Victoria's Heyday* which so well evokes what must have been the feel of England, particularly London, in the late 19th Century.

May Agate's rare little book mainly for the acting profession, *Madame Sarah*, was helpful and so too, of course, was Cornelia Otis Skinner's *Madame Sarah* which I think must be considered the definitive factual work on the subject of Sarah Bernhardt.

Alan Arnold

FOREWORD

Sarah Bernhardt (1844–1923), reputedly the greatest actress who ever lived, was an exceptional character in every way. She was unconventional to the point of eccentricity, ahead of her time in her social and intellectual attitudes, creative to the extent that she also became a fine sculptress and painter, ageless in the sense that she could play a young boy when she was already 56 and attract lovers half her age well into her 60s. In short, Sarah was driven by energies and insights which eventually made her great.

This is not a biography but a depiction of the actress's turbulent, formative years during which she overcame doubt, distress and fear in both her personal and professional life, laying the foundations for her greatness. It ends when she was 35, freed of everything but a talent that was to drive her through half a century into becoming the stuff of legend.

Her motto '*Quand Même*' expressed it, although it is not easily translatable into English – despite everything, no matter what, come what may? She refused to be defeated by life. Generations who have barely heard of her, to whom her legend is misted or unknown will, I hope, find in her story a passionate example of one person's victory over life.

HELEN M. STRAUSS

'Those who never saw her will only
be able to guess at it – but it
will be one of the most beautiful
and permanent guesses of mankind.'

Aubrey Baring

CHAPTER 1

Why, on that morning at her mother's house in the Rue St Honoré, was she awake so early thinking of wallflowers, flames and buckets of snow white milk? Clove-scented pinks and clumps of wallflowers, sad looking, the colour of Brittany's sunsets, the flowers of her childhood that had grown so profusely in the shade of the thatch-covered cottage at Quimperlé.

Flames. That never-to-be-forgotten day when, left alone by her nurse, she struggled in her high chair, tipped it over and fell into the fire! Only the cries for help from the nurse's paralysed husband who lay on the couch beside the opposite wall brought the nurse back from the field to snatch her from the fire and throw her all smoking into a bucket of milk.

Then from Paris in stage-coaches came her mother, aunts and a young doctor, a friend of her mother's, who approved of the masks of butter the Breton nurse and her neighbours were applying to her burned face. They had to be changed every two hours. To make these masks for the child so miraculously spared the villagers brought gifts of butter, and the house reeked of it. There was butter everywhere, on chairs, in cupboards, on tables and even on the bedsteads as well as in sheep's bladders hanging on the walls. She was only three at the time.

Now, at seventeen, these images from childhood were strong in Sarah's mind, recalling the terror of the flames, the smell of her scorched flesh, the cloy of butter on her skin, and the long weeks – forty-two days to be exact – of her recuperation. When the last bandage was removed there was not a scar to be seen, only faint marks which time would erase and heal leaving no more than shadows on her body. The villagers considered it a miracle. However, her mother took full credit. She distributed money on all sides to ensure that her daughter received from these simple country folk (who would have given it anyway) the attentions she herself had neglected to give during her long absences. Once she knew the crisis was over and after making arrangements for the child and the Breton nurse to live at a house in Neuilly on the banks of the Seine, Judith Bernhardt returned to her life in Paris.

. . . In the room in Rue St Honoré the light was strengthening, patterning the walls with the weave of the lace curtains. Sarah dreamed on. Yet was she dreaming? She was tensed to the day's beginnings, to a day that might prove to be the most important of her life, for on this day she was to be auditioned by the Director of the Comédie-Française. Was this why the past was coming back so clearly, reminding her of who she was and what had led up to this day of days? With half-opened eyes she saw that it was not yet six o'clock but it was impossible to sleep again. Her hands felt her body and she became less tense. It was such a slender body, skinny some said, but the fact did not displease her. On good days it was weightless with energy; only when she was depressed, which was not infrequent, was it a dead weight.

This particular day had to be a good one, she told herself, and in the warm protectiveness of her bed she willed it to be. She knew she was a creature of extremes, pitching between happiness so intense it was hardly bearable and periods of despair so deep they were dark nights of the soul. For this fact she blamed the circumstances of her childhood, especially the years at Neuilly.

At Neuilly she had been left alone for hour upon hour in the tiny walled garden full of dahlias growing so close together they looked like toy soldiers. She was moody and was often afraid, and at times wilful and destructive. The house was oppressed by the knowledge that the nurse's immobile husband was soon to die, and she felt constricted by its heavy silence to which her own speech, her tantrums, were a criminal affront. Twice she watched straw being strewn over the cobbles of the street to insulate the rumble of carriage wheels to give the stricken man extra quietude in death, but he did not die. She waited, a child of the shadows, for something to happen, something she hoped would be as dramatic though not as painful as falling in the fire but which would have the effect of bringing back her mother, her aunts and perhaps one or two of her mother's handsome friends to make her the centre of attention as she had been during those momentous days at Quimperlé. But her mother never came, the aunts never came, her nurse grew weary from tending the dying man, and although her mother sent money, bonbons and toys the years at Neuilly were spent waiting to be taken away from that depressing house where the hall clock chimed the hours pessimistically through two damp winters.

When Sarah was five something did happen. The husband died and the Breton woman remarried with minimal delay the caretaker of an important house in the Rue de Provence and there she proposed to live with him. The nurse had never been taught to write, but in any case the whereabouts of Sarah's mother were at this time unknown. She was travelling and the funds for Sarah's upkeep had arrived from various places, most recently from Baden-Baden. So the Breton moved to her new spouse's home taking Sarah with her.

The conciergerie comprised two rooms above the entrance to the house in the Rue de Provence. On arrival there on a grey November afternoon Sarah, happy in her release from Neuilly, thought how beautiful and safe it looked from the outside with its huge round window above the ornamental door. Tired from the excitements of the journey she was put to bed and went to sleep at once. But when she awoke it was to the realization that the tiny room in which she had slept had no window at all. Struggling from the arms of her nurse, who was dressing her, she ran into the adjoining room and pressed her brow against the big round window, but there were no trees in sight, no hint of green, nothing but the bleak ugliness of stone. 'I want to go away,' she screamed. 'I don't want to stay here. It is all black, black and ugly. I want to see the ceiling of the street.' The nurse wrapped a blanket round the weeping child's shoulders, took her hand and led her into the courtyard. 'Now, Milk-blossom,' she said, 'look up and you will see the ceiling of the street.' Sarah looked up and saw the sky.

As she remembered that bitter day her heart sank even now, for light had always been important to her, light and space; she could endure silence and be alone but she could not stand being caged. But as it was vital to avoid a depression on this most important of days, she shifted her thoughts from that windowless cell in the Rue de Provence and recalled instead the remarkable circumstances of her leaving it . . .

One day she was sitting alone on the curb outside the imposing house pretending that a leaf afloat in the water of the guttering was a sailing ship when a carriage broke down opposite where she sat. She watched the coachman dismount and pick up a bit of broken harness. Her eyes were sullen and she did not brighten when the coachman smiled. But when she saw the passenger her face lit up at once. It was Aunt Rosine! In no time at all she shot up from the gutter, rushed over to the landau and flinging her muddy arms out wide made an impassioned plea to be taken away. So startled was the woman that she did not immediately recognize the street urchin whose filthy hands were now clawing at the expensive whipcord upholstery of the elegant coach, but once recovered she stepped down hurriedly, relieved to see the Breton nurse hurrying in their direction. The nurse pulled the yelling child away, marched her back to the house and shut the door on her. Yet before the nurse had finished apologizing to the aunt for what had happened they were appalled to see the child fall to earth a few feet away from them. She had somehow managed to open the round window and jump from it. At this the aunt relented and with the help of the coachman bundled the half-conscious child into the carriage and took her home. She never saw her Breton nurse again.

. . . If fate had ever shown its hand, Sarah reflected as she lay fully awake now in her mother's house, it had done so then. With all Paris to break down in why should Aunt Rosine's carriage have done so then and there if not due to something more than mere coincidence?

Aunt Rosine's problem was to find her sister Judith and persuade the reluctant mother to take better care of the child. But Sarah's broken limbs had healed before Rosine established contact with her sister. Eventually, Judith was discovered to be unusually well set up in a stylish apartment in the Rue de la Michodière, and arrangements were made for Sarah's transfer there.

Judith Bernhardt, half Jewish, half Dutch, had come to Paris from Holland after becoming pregnant by a young law student. She had money to tide her over and after giving birth to Sarah she placed her in the charge of the wet-nurse at Quimperlé. Returning then to Paris she determinedly set about one of the few ways of making a living open to unmarried women without families or fortunes in the mid-nineteenth century. She became a *courtisane*, a respectable prostitute. Under Louis-Philippe, then in his seventies, Paris had the liveliest demi-monde in Europe. For many a married man of good social position a mistress was a status symbol and for a married woman tolerance of that mistress was often the price to be paid for retaining her husband and home. Beyond being a milliner, a dressmaker or a governess – or, if talented, a career in the theatre – there was little scope for a single woman and being kept was a means of livelihood for many. Judith Bernhardt, handsome, astute and fond of luxury, was well suited to such a life-style. She had a gift for making young men feel important and important men feel young, and gradually she acquired some wealthy and influential patrons. Freedom was essential to this particular way of life and she was very reluctant to compromise herself by becoming a full-time parent. Her daughter, she knew, was strong-willed, sensitive and demanding and would be a grave handicap to her. Yet in response to Rosine's appeals she was determined to try, and for three years mother and daughter lived under the same roof.

In this situation Sarah grew still more moody. She loved her mother and thought her glamorous and beautiful but she was often shut out, especially when she watched Judith preparing for an evening with a client, her body becoming taut as it reacted to each hated crimp and press of the curling irons as her mother endlessly preened and titivated herself, leaving the child sullen and accusatory. There were days when her mother petted and indulged her, others when she felt excluded entirely from affection. Sometimes, when her mother said good night, she would turn her face away, sleep fitfully, wait for the sound of the latch-key that meant her mother had come home. No one more than Judith felt relieved when it was decided that Sarah should go to a boarding-school.

Her years at Madame Fressard's Academy for Young Ladies at Auteuil, Sarah later realized, were those in which she had begun to find an identity. For the first time she had the companionship of girls of her own age and although they made fun of her thinness and crinkly red hair she could fight back. Years of self-dependence had given her a certain inner toughness; she could be hard, vicious even, and fly into tempers so convulsive that those around her became wary of upsetting her again. For these demonic spells she compensated with an ability to charm, which so impressed the patient Madame Fressard that she predicted in her private diary that for Sarah fate held two alternatives – triumph or tragedy – nothing in between. She was a child of the light or of the darkness, the teacher believed, but no longer of the shadows. The truth of this seemed to be underlined when she took part in a school production of a playlet entitled *Clothilde* in which she was cast as the Queen of the Fairies. When the child Clothilde heartlessly declares in front of the Fairy Queen a total disbelief in fairies, causing the Queen to die of shock, Sarah's collapse into death was so realistic that it brought gasps of terror from the audience.

Thinking back upon those school years Sarah realized that she had not been unhappy. True, there had been the fits of rage provoked by the taunts of other girls, fits so cataleptic in nature that it took the combined strength of Madame Fressard and the gardener's boy to restrain her, but they had become less frequent as her self-possession grew. Judith visited only twice, but surprisingly Sarah had not missed her mother. They wrote to each other but already Sarah had become secretive, keeping back the things which really mattered in her life, like the time in the countryside around the school when she had won a dare. Her companions had dared her to jump across a ditch far too wide for an apparently rather frail girl of nine to leap. Summoning every ounce of strength, willing herself to accomplish the feat, she had flown up like some metamorphosized demon, splashing down within an inch of the far side, yelling in flight the motto she had adopted for herself, '*Quand même!*' She suffered a mere sprain of an ankle.

Quand même – In spite of everything. It was applicable now, Sarah reminded herself, to the challenge she had to meet at the Comédie-Française, and as she lay awake in her mother's house waiting for the day to begin she spoke aloud the piece she had prepared for the audition: 'Once upon a time, there were two pigeons . . .'

The day would begin with the arrival of Mam'selle – Mme Guérard – who would fuss around with her usual self-effacing concern. Dear Mam'selle. But for this melancholy rather old-fashioned woman, whom she had come to love so deeply, Sarah believed that she would have failed to shed the insecurities which dogged her even after the years at Madame Fressard's. For as she became more self-aware her curiosity about her beginnings grew – where had she been born? Where was her father? What had he looked like? – questions which Judith never satisfactorily answered. Her mother gave her several highly imaginative accounts. One told of her birth at Le Havre during Judith's brief but tragic marriage to a Belgian marquess who had been killed while mountaineering in Switzerland. Another version depicted her as the daughter of an American diplomat who had died at the hands of assassins in Bombay. Judith's mind seemed to spawn variations on the theme of Sarah's beginnings with increasing fertility as her fortunes increased; by the time she had attained a secure social position with a fine home in the Rue St Honoré and friends of unquestionable influence and power Judith would account for Sarah only if pressed to do so and then in the most bizarre and colourful terms. 'You are the daughter of one of the most eminent oculists in Germany,' she had once informed her daughter, 'who died of fish poisoning in Peking while on a visit to China to cure a dynastic prince of glaucoma.' But after Mam'selle came into her life as her first tutor Sarah made no further enquiries. She would spend hours in Mam'selle's little flat, which during her adolescence became a retreat from Judith's gay parties and receptions, in the company of this gentle, wise widow who gave her the next best thing to a mother's love. From Madame Guérard, whom she had always called Mam'selle, she learnt that she had a right to be herself.

Sarah believed she owed to Mam'selle more even than

to Mother St Sophie, the Superior at the Convent of Grand-Champ at Versailles at which she had been installed at the age of ten on the advice of the influential Duc de Morny, one of her mother's closest friends. She took to religion as to a drug. Its symbols and ceremonials, the mystery of the Mass, was a theatricality to which she could relate both body and mind. The chantings, the incense, the holy water, the use of candlelight, above all the cross were the props of a drama so intense that she was irresistibly drawn into it. The fits she had experienced at Madame Fressard's sometimes recurred but they were far less frequent, and the kindness of the nuns, in particular the influence of Mother St Sophie, whose healing hands brought calm when the fits occurred, so influenced her that for some time she believed that in the mysticism of the Roman Catholic Church she had found her final home. Even the spartan dignity of the convent pleased her. She was given a portion of garden in which to grow flowers and herbs and she was allowed to keep small pets, but her taste in these upset the nuns for she kept death-watch beetles, spiders, lizards and adders and crickets gathered from the garden leaves. 'Wouldn't you like instead to keep butterflies or a cage-bird?' the Mother Superior enquired. Sarah replied to the effect that she preferred to love what was considered ugly and unlovable. The whole world loved what was beautiful, she said, an outlook the holy Mother took to be a sign that the child had in her the stuff of religious commitment – and became ambitious for her to adopt the church as a vocation.

Inevitably, Sarah went too far in her enthusiasm. Her fervour got out of hand. One icy February night she slipped from her dormitory bed at Grand-Champ wearing only her nightdress intent on a solitary commune with the Archangel Raphael in the chapel. Next morning the young fanatic was found half-frozen in the unheated sanctuary from which she was rushed to hospital. The doctors diagnosed pneumonia and for some time it was thought she would die. She recovered sufficiently to enjoy being the centre of family attention again. Her mother, summoned from Paris, arrived with a young widow who was to take her to recuperate at Cauterets in the Pyrenees. From the moment they met Sarah knew that they were to become indispensable to one another – for this was her first meeting with Mam'selle.

Despite Mam'selle's devoted care Sarah's recovery was slow and the illness left her with a hacking cough. She was fifteen and now regarded as constitutionally frail. She was unlikely to live beyond a few years, the doctors agreed. When their opinion became known to Sarah she adopted the tragic pose with unmitigated enthusiasm and determined to extract from the situation the maximum attention from her family. If need be death would be embraced with the same fervour she had applied to her religious obsessions. Doomed to an early demise she would live the part to full effect so that when her Aunt Rosine paid a visit she asked if she might be taken on a tour of the public mortuaries. To her mother she put a request so alarming that it froze that life-loving woman. 'I want you to buy me a coffin,' she said. 'I would like it now so that I may get used to it.' The request was refused but she so pestered her mother that Judith, anxious for a quiet life, bought her one and it was placed in Sarah's room. To Judith's stark distaste Sarah occasionally rested in it!

But she was not content to surround herself with the morbid appurtenances of death. She terrified the household by two attempts to provide the one missing item – a corpse. Both efforts to end her life were so inept that they could not but fail. One involved the drinking of a bottle of ink, which merely made her sick. The other, preceded by some highly dramatic farewell notes to members of her family, was to take the form of a leap from her bedroom window but was frustrated by Mam'selle's habit of locking the shutters. Obviously, Judith needed the sort of help with

Sarah that neither her family nor even the kindly tutor could give, the firm hand a feminine household sometimes lacks, a father figure. Meanwhile, the energy Sarah applied to her flirtations with death drained Judith's *joie de vivre.* With all her heart she began to regret the absence of a masculine presence and being a woman of resource she decided to do something about it. She called a conference in her living-room to which the aunts were invited but more significantly she asked four of her most trusted male friends to attend. They were men of substance and included an old flame with whom she had had a love affair that had matured over the years into a valued friendship, the Duc de Morny. Also present was an attorney from Le Havre.

Sarah, whom her mother had expected to appear miserably overwrought, impressed everyone by her calmness and dignity. Wearing a dress of blue silk which suited her slimness she was a picture of composure. Judith and her sisters relaxed but the Duc, who had a soft spot for Sarah, looked on wryly, prepared for anything. It was the attorney who sparked it off. This gold-spectacled, smoothly sinister-looking man discomfited her the moment she set eyes on him, and the distaste was mutual. When coffee had been drunk and the cups taken away he coughed nervously and addressed her. 'As your mother will have told you,' he began loftily, 'we are meeting today to discuss your future . . .' Sarah's body stiffened, the Duc grew wary . . . 'but first it should be made clear that a sum of money, which you will inherit when you marry, was put aside for you by your father, who died in Pisa . . .'

'That's a lie,' said Sarah.

Although ruffled, the attorney chose to ignore the remark, cleared his throat and was about to resume when Sarah burst upon him again. 'He did not die in Pisa. He was shot in Texas by anti-abolitionists. And I will not marry. I'll marry the Lord our God. I want to be a nun.'

'Sarah!' shouted Judith.

'Ah, indeed,' said the urbane Duc while Aunt Rosine tutted.

'You have to be rich to enter a convent,' snarled the attorney, 'and you haven't got a sou.'

'I have my father's money.'

'Not unless you marry,' said the attorney. 'It is for the purpose of getting you married.'

'Nuns marry the Saviour,' retorted Sarah.

The attorney raised his hands in hopelessness and appealed to the company for support. But Sarah had rushed over to her mother. 'You don't mind my being a nun, do you? Would it make you unhappy?' Judith said it would. She then went from one to another imploring each to help, begging passionately for understanding, capping her lobbyings with a high-pitched, histrionic plea. 'I will never marry for money. My heart is with the Lord. I am the daughter of the divine Mary, the mother of us all . . .'

'And half Jewish into the bargain,' snapped the attorney, a remark that stopped the child in her tracks. The malice of it caused Judith to wince. Then the Duc acted. He rose, seemingly bored, but turned and spoke to Judith. 'One thing is clear,' he said. 'Sarah must go to the Conservatoire.' He kissed Judith tenderly, patted Sarah's cheek and bowed to the others. Before leaving he spoke to everyone there in a tone of quiet authority. 'Follow my advice and send her to the Conservatoire,' he said. 'She is a born actress.'

Now with deep affection Sarah remembered him – aristocratic, sceptical, dapper, a man of enormous influence in France, the half-brother of the Emperor Louis-Napoleon and his closest confidant. What an incredible achievement on the part of her mother to have persuaded this distinguished figure to spend two hours in their cramped, bourgeois surroundings to listen to a debate about her future. Because of the respect in which he was held what he had said had carried the weight of an edict. She was to be an actress. But the idea had then seemed repugnant. At the convent she had once seen the famous actress Rachel, who had visited the place. Mother St Sophie had conducted her on a tour of the garden. Rachel, old and frail, had become out of breath and had had to sit down. A nun had brought medicine to revive the celebrated lady. She looked deathly pale. Later one of the sisters told Sarah that Rachel had lived a life of wickedness and for this God was punishing her. Was the Duc serious in his opinion or just amusing himself when he made that statement at the family conference? Reassurance came later in the day. A member of the Duc's staff brought Judith a message – the Duc's box at the Comédie was available to them, it said, and the note concluded: 'Take her to the theatre this evening and I believe your worries will be over. A girl like that has stars in her eyes. I sincerely believe her kingdom of heaven lies not in a nunnery but in the theatre.'

What a day that had been! After dinner Sarah, her mother and Mam'selle squeezed into a cab and set off for the Comédie-Française. Installed in the splendid, crested box Sarah felt Mam'selle's sharp knees pressing through the velvet back of her chair, and was comforted for she had never been to a theatre before. When the curtain rose on *Amphytrion* she thought she would faint with excitement. This was not just a play; she had read plays at school. It was a completely different world in which people lived lives beyond the everyday, a world of light and space where time itself was in the hands of conjurors. Its possibilities were limitless. It was an infinity in which figures floated intangibly, voices were incantations and movement had about it the gravity of a religious ritual. When the curtain fell she knew that it was the only world capable of absorbing her restless energy, her fears, her sadnesses, her deepest joys. In that world she would live a thousand lives.

The National Conservatory of Music and Declaration provided a two-year course which Sarah undertook with the greatest of zeal. With Mam'selle she walked there each day, saving the francs her mother gave her for the horse-drawn omnibus so as to be able at the end of some days to treat her companion to a cab ride home. She did not miss a single lesson and often she rehearsed her diction in her bedroom until late at night. At last, Judith felt, a channel had been found for the tempestuous life-force of her difficult daughter. The family backed her to the hilt, aunts deluging her with volumes of Racine, Corneille and Molière which, perversely, she barely opened; she did not understand them. Instead she read the fables of La Fontaine which she loved passionately and knew so well that she could actually recite them backwards.

Sarah's chief tutor at the Conservatoire for the first year was Monsieur Provost, who had spent thirty years at the Comédie-Française and was considered one of the finest actors of his day. Provost fell ill and she was taken over for the second year by Monsieur Samson, a teacher of genius who had taught many successful players including the unique Rachel whom he discovered when she was a street singer. Sarah at first believed in him wholeheartedly. However, they clashed at the end of the Conservatoire course over his choice of examination pieces. These examinations were vitally important. Success meant a trial engagement at either the Comédie-Française or the Théâtre Royal de l'Odéon. Samson selected as an exercise in comedy an excerpt from Delavigne's *L'Ecole des veillards* and as an exercise in tragedy one from the same author's *La Fille du Cid.* Although only seventeen and not well read, her instinct already told her that although Delavigne had been revered in his prime twenty years earlier his verse-style had become stuffy and outmoded. The choices gave little chance for her to show her talent. But Samson could not be persuaded and Sarah studied the dull lines with a heavy heart.

On examination day she did her best, but failed badly in the tragic piece by reason of never having been able to believe in it, but she went into the comedy piece with indefatigable grit and played it with such wit and style that it earned her a second prize. But only a first prize would have satisfied Judith. After the examination Sarah, her mother and Mam'selle returned to the Rue St Honoré in silence. In Judith's view two years of hope and sacrifice had come to nothing; why hadn't she insisted that her daughter accept the proposal of marriage a year ago from a wealthy silk merchant who had travelled all the way from Amsterdam to make it? Now there would be further tantrums from Sarah, more morose silences, further responsibility to find another solution. For both their sakes she wanted Sarah to be independent. She could not go on using her friends on her daughter's behalf or have the atmosphere of her home taken over by this self-centred child. It was spoiling her own enjoyment of life.

For several days Judith's fears were justified. Sarah was inconsolable. When not laid out like a sleeping swan amid the satin linings of her rosewood coffin she moped about with an aimlessness so contrary to her mother's purposeful nature that Judith wished the wretched child were anywhere but in her home. Such feelings were doubly upsetting to Judith because they were at odds with her sense of compassion, for there were times when she looked at her daughter and wanted to weep. Sarah was so vulnerable; they both were. Then something happened which changed that abode of gloom into one of sheer delight – and caused Judith to say a prayer of gratitude for the friendship of the Duc de Morny. For he alone could have been responsible for the arrival by special delivery of a letter bearing the seal of the Comédie-Française, and signed by Edouard Thierry, its administrator. The letter invited Sarah to present herself for an audition.

By the clock on her bedside table she saw that it was eight o'clock. From the street came the rumble of an early omnibus, the chink of milk urns. Soon Mam'selle would come down from her tiny flat to collect fresh croissants from the local bakery, bringing them with a brown jug of hot chocolate to her room. It was a spring morning to revitalize the senses and as she rose to meet it Sarah let the ghosts of the past return to where she could not be reached by them and prepared her mind for the audition at the Comédie-Française.

CHAPTER 2

The Comédie-Française or Théâtre-Français, the French state theatre, was founded in the seventeenth century in honour of Molière, France's great actor-playwright. Its players formed a kind of co-operative of *sociétaires* who determined the policy and shared the profits of the theatre. Winners of first prizes at the Paris Conservatoire had the right to an audition there but even if they were successful enough to be asked to join the Comédie for a trial period they would not be invited to become a *sociétaire*; a player waited years for that distinction. Once elected, however, nothing could dislodge them and after thirty years a *sociétaire* had the right to retire on a pension. A theatre run by *sociétaires*, by its very nature and constitution, was bound to favour policies that were safe rather than adventurous so that while the great institution was covered in past glory it was also the despair of those who believed in breaking new ground.

No one was more aware of the theatre's failings than the conservatively dressed, unsmiling man with eyes that long ago had lost their fire who sat listening to the hopefuls from the Conservatoire. These yearly auditions were among the least enjoyable duties expected from Edouard Thierry, the theatre's director. In the course of a long career he had not discovered from them a single talent to thrill the senses. Plenty of competence, of course, but nothing unique, exciting; and he blamed in part the rigidities of the Conservatoire's classically-based teaching policy. He also blamed himself for having failed over the years to free the Comédie from its stifling enslavement to tradition. Sometimes it seemed to him that nothing had changed, from the stylized acting to the conceptions of set design, from the time of

Molière two hundred years ago. At first he had fought hard to give the Comédie a bright new image but the *sociétaires* had defeated him and in time he too had opted for conformity.

Earlier in his career, years ago, he would sometimes get away from the Comédie's incestuous atmosphere of gossip and spite and visit secretly, alone, some of the little back-street theatres, two or three in a single evening. During such explorations sometimes, very rarely, he would come across the suspicion of a talent, rough-hewn, untouched, sensual, and yearn to chance his arm, but knowing how the *sociétaires* would react he had played safe and left well alone, despising himself. The French theatre so sorely needed fresh spirit. For against the backdrop of Louis-Napoleon's imperial façade society was divided. Many Frenchmen loathed its sham and reactionary features, including its heavy censorship, and longed for an atmosphere in which the arts might be free. Yet the established players at the Comédie lived in a world of their own. They were jealous of each other and hostile to innovation. Over the years Thierry too had settled for the two things which in a *métier* as fickle as the theatre were all but irresistible: security and prestige. These the Comédie certainly afforded. He loved the old theatre, nevertheless, and had not totally lost hope. Before he retired something might happen to make him feel that he had contributed more than years of time-serving to this most transient of the arts.

But what was happening on the stage in the empty theatre now would not strengthen that belief – a young actress, a fledgling from the Conservatoire, was causing him great pain by her interpretation, if such it could be called, of a passage from a play by Racine.

'Nero watched me with fearsome looks, his eyes never leaving mine, watching for the merest gesture, the smallest word . . .' Not only was the aspirant's voice nerve-jangling – she was over-acting. '. . . So if our love I did betray, his vengeance would fall swiftly on you, my love.' Mine will fall on you if you are not careful, thought Thierry, his hand moving to the little brass bell which he rang to stop an audition. But he decided to give her a little longer, for doubtless her mother was listening proudly in the wings. 'Ah, how oft I was about to show mine anguish unto thee! How many sighs I checked upon my lips, shunning thine eyes the while, that mine were ever fain to seek!' Did Racine really write this rubbish? Thierry was always amazed how a bad performance could make even classic verse sound nonsensical. Yet great acting could elevate trivia into the realms of the sublime. Now the girl's companion, a young man to feed her with cue lines, began to read. 'Ah, this is all too much, too much to hear . . .' To which the girl responded : 'With one's beloved, what torture not to speak!'

Thierry's hand took up the bell and shook it testily. 'Thank you, thank you,' he said, and to his secretary: 'Rejected.'

The stage was set for a garden scene in the play to be performed that night. How seedy it looked in the full flood of the audition lighting, Thierry thought. Warily, he looked about him, scanning the rows of gilt and crimson boxes from which night after night Parisians surveyed one another more attentively than they watched the play. Was this what theatre was all about? Of course not. Nor would there be any change, he knew, while personalities like Madame Nathalie reigned in his company. She had the arrogance of a pampered duchess, he decided as he looked at her now, for there she sat in the stalls three rows in front of him, huge, condescending and very over-dressed, the principal actress of the Comédie. A critic had once called her 'Nathalie the fat, the solemn, the old and wicked *sociétaire*' and without doubt she represented the Comédie's worst faults : complacency and refusal to accept change. She was jealous of new talent, opposed every hint at innovation and paid a claque to maintain the myth of her magnetism. Thierry despaired. The auditions had been going on for hours but even should the faintest shadow of talent reveal itself on that stage this ridiculous woman would do her best to sabotage it. He leaned back and wondered how much more he could take. 'Next,' he called.

A stagehand appeared from the wings. 'Mademoiselle Sarah Bernhardt,' he announced. Thierry looked dully at her for in appearance she was not encouraging: a rather shapeless body, far too thin, a mop of unruly red hair and the virginal white dress the Conservatoire insisted upon. His mind prepared for yet another assault. Nathalie, however, appeared unusually interested. Normally, the cantankerous actress would munch chocolates or fidget, but she was peering at this girl through opera-glasses. What could Nathalie possibly see in her? She was certainly not beautiful.

'I am Monsieur Thierry, the director of the theatre,' he said mechanically to the girl on the stage. Then he indicated Nathalie so intently regarding her. 'And this is Madame Nathalie, our principal actress. Where is your partner, Mademoiselle?'

'Partner?'

'Yes, to read your cues to you.'

Sarah cleared her throat. 'I have no partner.'

'Weren't you told that for an audition at the Comédie-Française you were expected to prepare a scene?'

'No, sir.' Panic was on the verge of setting in.

Thierry was distinctly irritated. Applicants should at least have the courtesy to prepare themselves properly. Stage-struck nonentities. Then it crossed his mind that this could be the girl the Duc de Morny had mentioned to him. He was known to have a penchant for the young. But was this unformed, inept-looking creature really his latest plaything? The Duc's tastes were surprising, thought Thierry. 'What *have* you prepared?' he asked.

'A fable.'

Thierry despaired. 'A fable?'

'I shall recite the fable of the *Two Pigeons* by La Fontaine.'

Stupefied, he told her to begin. 'All right.'

Sarah moved to the centre of the stage; she bowed and began diminuitively. 'Once upon a time there were two pigeons who loved each other dearly, as brothers do . . .'

'Louder, Mademoiselle, louder,' Thierry called and Sarah became confused. The unfriendliness, the restless presence of the large woman below her were causing her acute discomfort. She wanted to bolt. 'Come, come,' said Thierry. 'We're not ogres. Begin again and speak up.'

'Once upon a time . . .'

'If she's to begin again,' said Nathalie, finding humour in the situation, 'it will take longer than an excerpt from a play.' She heaved herself round to face Thierry and she was smiling. Bitch, thought Thierry.

The intrusion angered Sarah. It aroused her combative spirit. For several moments she looked at Nathalie with eyes of steel. She began again. This time her voice was strong and her presence composed.

'Once upon a time there were two pigeons, who loved each other deeply, as brothers do. But one of them grew tired of the familiar hills and valleys of their country and yearned to explore the world far, far away . . .' Her voice embraced the theatre mellifluously, word flowing into word as in an incantation. 'No sooner had he set off than a storm overtook him. Soaked through, he sought the shelter of a tree, but suddenly found himself caught in a net. Bird catchers had spied on him . . .'

As the little parable proceeded it began to sound profound. Nathalie, no longer smiling, lowered her opera-glasses, people listened from the wings and an old cleaning woman put down her brushes and sat in the stalls. Thierry's eyes, fixed steadily on Sarah, conveyed nothing.

Sarah continued : 'Struggling, he broke through the mesh and flew away. But hardly had he escaped when a vulture swooped down from the heavens and attacked him!' Thierry was being held by every word. Did the girl really know what she was doing? It seemed preposterous that at her age she could convey suffering as if she knew what that was all about!

'Diving lower to escape the hungry bird, he found himself a target for a boy with a sling who hit him with a stone.' The voice conveyed the pity, the sadness of it. Thierry pulled himself together – the girl had probably worked on the piece for weeks. First impressions were often fatal. His thoughts travelled back over the years, to his prowls around the narrow, winding streets of old Paris. He recalled the voices of the poor, so different from fashionable stage diction, and saw again their strained hungry faces. How could this girl on the stage in front of him in her simple white dress reciting a sentimental fable know anything about adversity or how it felt to be deprived?

'Half dead, his wings and feathers torn, he limped home to his brother. How happy they were to see each other. They . . .' Thierry picked up his bell and shook it fretfully. Sarah looked surprised. She turned to go. 'One moment, mademoiselle.' Thierry consulted his list. 'Mademoiselle Bernhardt.' She stood still. 'That was not at all bad,' he said. 'Accepted.'

She wanted to leap the footlights and hug him. Instead, she fled to the wings where Mam'selle had waited. Together they ran to the stage door. The Rue St Honoré was within walking distance but Judith had insisted on a carriage to give her daughter confidence.

'Wait until Mama hears,' said Sarah.

'I knew it,' said Mam'selle. 'I was sure you would.'

'Mother *never* believed I would.' Mam'selle detected danger signals. Sarah, no longer smiling, was in a mood to be perverse. The carriage drew up at the house and

Mam'selle was soon standing on the pavement calling up to Judith who had appeared at a first-floor window. 'She did it, Madame,' she called. 'She did it. She's accepted.' Sarah was furious. She caught up with her companion and pummelled her. 'What are you saying! I told you I was going to surprise her.' She reached the front door as her mother opened it. 'Sarah, my dear, how wonderful!' Judith exclaimed.

'Go back in,' Sarah said sternly. 'Go back in, Mother, and pretend you know nothing about it.'

'What?'

'I am going to make my entrance as I planned,' said Sarah.

Judith glanced at Mam'selle breathless from the climb. They understood she had to be indulged. 'Go in, I said,' Sarah commanded. 'And don't come out until I knock.'

Judith closed the door. Mam'selle climbed the stairs to her own apartment. Sarah knocked. The door opened. 'Oh, Sarah, it's you,' said Judith. 'How was your audition?' Games like this didn't really appeal to her but patiently she followed Sarah into the living-room.

'Mother, it was terrible,' said Sarah. 'I walked on stage and they asked me to do a scene but I hadn't prepared one. I said I would do a fable and they laughed! They talked all through my recitation! Several times they made me stop. They even said they couldn't hear me!'

'My poor child,' said Judith. 'Poor, poor child.' It was the only way, Judith knew, to get it over. Why couldn't her daughter be more adult! She looked apologetically at the Duc de Morny whose presence Sarah had not even acknowledged, but was reassured to see him smiling.

'It was humiliating,' continued Sarah. 'Mortifying!'

'Now you mustn't take it so badly,' said Judith.

'They rang the bell before I had finished!'

'My poor Sarah.'

'They rang the bell . . . to tell me I was *accepted*!'

'Accepted? Why, Sarah, how clever of you.' The performance was over. Judith retired to the sofa exhausted but she summoned the energy to say to the Duc, 'Isn't it marvellous, my dear Duc?' Then she sagged back into the cushions.

'The Comédie-Française! I congratulate you, Sarah,' said the Duc. He was genuinely pleased.

'I was magnificent!' said Sarah. 'They loved me. I stood on the stage all alone. I *made* them listen. They couldn't take their eyes off me. And I am going to be the greatest actress who ever lived!' At that she rushed from the room with all the force of a seabird diving in a following wind. Judith suddenly felt very old, tired and dispirited, and hoped the Duc would not notice. But the Duc had noticed and he understood. He knew well how Judith felt. He had spent the morning with Louis-Napoleon whose obsession with destiny was just as trying. From meetings with the Emperor he invariably emerged limp. So he went over to Judith and kissed her very gently. But the Duc's compassionate kiss disturbed her; she mistook it for a gesture of pity. She valued his respect above that of any of her friends, for she had known him longest. He was the most powerful, the most illustrious of her conquests, and she resented, as she so often did, her daughter's ability to make her feel old and vulnerable. It was pure selfishness. Sarah thought that everyone existed solely for her, accessories to her whims, and was quite incapable of realizing that others had hopes and aspirations too. It was stupid of her ever to have allowed Sarah to live with her. It had, she believed, cost her a proposal of marriage from the Duc, for they were certainly in love at the time. Sarah should have remained, Judith believed, a skeleton in the cupboard. Instead she had become an overwhelming presence in the parlour, and was more difficult to live with as time went by. Only Sarah could make her feel old, used, insecure; her daughter lived in a world of fantasy and no one knew what she would do next.

'She will disgrace me,' Judith said to the Duc. 'I know she will.'

De Morny smiled. How conveniently she had forgotten the nature of her own rise to respectability. 'It's not a bad occupation being an actress and she certainly has the imagination for it.'

'That's the trouble,' Judith said irritably. 'She can't tell the difference between reality and make-believe.'

'Now, come, that's not altogether fair.'

'You take her side as if you were her father,' Judith snapped. Her tone had malice in it too.

The Duc considered this. He was fond of Judith but wished she would not be so obsessional about Sarah. 'I take a paternal interest in her,' he said. 'We *all* do. I and your other gentlemen friends.' It was easy to deflate her.

'I'm sure I appreciate that, my dear Duc,' she said, humbled, 'but how can she become an actress with that face and that hair and that figure?'

The Duc was bored with the subject. 'Anyway,' he said, 'the theatrical profession has its advantages. It will keep her out of the house at night.'

They smiled.

On reaching her bedroom Sarah shared her triumph with her pets – a tiny lizard, a turtle and a butterfly in a jar. 'I won!' she announced to them in turn. Then to a statue of the Virgin Mary on the wall above her bed she said: 'Blessed Virgin, please forgive me – I can't take the veil.' She knelt. 'I must *act*, you see. I was *born* to act – even though I promised you I'd be a nun. You do understand, don't you, my beautiful, my blessed Mary? I shall always love you.' She kissed the statue. 'But wait until you see me on the stage.'

While she knelt she became aware of voices from the sitting-room. Her mother's voice was strident. 'She will disgrace me.' Sarah went rigid. 'How can she become an actress with that face and that hair and that figure?' It was a betrayal. Wouldn't anything satisfy her mother?

Hadn't she just proved herself? Her mood hardened and she found no comfort in the Virgin Mary. Instead, the cold beady stare of the motionless lizard took her fancy. She picked it up and ran to the living-room.

'Mother, I have a present for you,' she announced. 'Close your eyes. Let me pin it on.'

Judith moved from the Duc's arms. 'Why, thank you, Sarah,' she said and allowed her daughter to pin to her breast the inert lizard on a chain. Then it moved, darting frenziedly into the cleft of her bosom. 'My God, it's alive,' Judith screamed and tried to brush it off, tearing at her dress, finally hurling the lizard to the floor. 'How could you! You and your horrible crawling creatures!' She was in tears. But Sarah wasn't listening; she was interested in the lizard. On picking it up she realized it was dead. 'You've killed it!' she said, spitting the words at her mother venomously as she ran from the room.

Judith looked despairingly at de Morny who took her into his arms. 'What am I to do?' she asked. 'What will become of her?' But they were questions she had asked before and there were, she knew, no answers.

CHAPTER 3

Judith's opinion of her daughter's appearance was not shared by Sarah or by others who knew her. She did not assess herself in the same way. When she was depressed she felt ugly and dark inside and no amount of looking in a mirror would rekindle the light. It had to come from within. But when she was happy she was so marvellously alive that whether she was beautiful or not did not cross the minds of those about her. Judith alone was blind to her daughter's power to magnetize because she had suffered too much from the girl's extravagant and unpredictable changes of mood. For Sarah could be radiant with thrusting energy one day, a burnt-out candle the next. Judith's opinion was the product of exasperation and fatigue and Sarah's rejection of it a necessary part of her defence against loss of confidence. If she had believed her mother for a moment she would have been conscious always of an Achilles heel for, in truth, Judith was right – Sarah was far from beautiful.

She was of average height but the slightness of her build and in particular the slenderness of her waist made her look a little taller. She had a firm chin, a rather aquiline nose and high cheekbones. Her eyes were widely spaced and exceptionally blue, her mouth full and unusually red against the pallor of her skin. It was her hair that most expressed her tempestuous and spirited nature; it was almost negroid: frizzy, unruly, hard to comb, the bane of hairdressers who had to tug at it for hours to give it order and shape. It was red-gold. She wore gold-coloured things to match it. Gold was her favourite colour. So first impressions were of the hair and her slimness. When not burdened by the voluminous fashions of the day, which she disliked intensely, she looked unbelievably slender. Tight waists were another dislike because they made her look wraith-like. But constricting clothes were psychologically objectionable because her body still bore the faint marks of the burning at Quimperlé. Although these were painless they were stamped upon her mind like brands, never to be touched.

During the summer of '62 Sarah prepared for her professional debut. Relations with her mother reflected her new feeling of purpose. At week-ends they would sometimes drive to the Bois de Boulogne, the royal forest which Louis-Napoleon had given to the people of Paris, or to Longchamps to see what progress was being made in the creation there of a racecourse. This had been the Duc de Morny's idea; he wanted to create at Longchamps a fashionable social resort the profits from which would pay for the landscaping of the Bois into a people's park. Paris, like Sarah's life, was undergoing sea-change, a fundamental transformation in pursuit of which there was construction everywhere – culminating in the majesty of the Arc de Triomphe. All this was in the hands of Louis-Napoleon's brilliant, ruthless Prefect of the Seine, the Alsatian-born Baron Georges Eugène Haussmann, who was well on the way to providing Paris with some eighty-five miles of new streets with wide carriage-ways lined with trees. Impressive railway stations were arising, as were great hotels and department stores. At Les Halles splendid in metal and glass stood the new central vegetable market. Still far from finished, the palatial new Opera was being criticized for its pretentious opulence.

Judith believed in the Second Empire unreservedly. France was coming into her glory again. Sarah did not. She had reservations concerning Napoleon III's obsession with grandeur, but the two women seldom discussed the subject; it only confirmed Judith in her conviction that her daughter was by nature perverse or exasperated Sarah who spurned her mother's bourgeois values. At their extremes she considered them nothing short of hypocritical. It was clear that all was far from well with France, so deeply was she committed to conflicting alliances and so unwisely entangled with aggressions in China, Africa and Mexico. While the masses in Paris and the whole of France lived in terrible poverty Louis-Napoleon was building an ostentatious panoply of false power.

That summer Sarah read the great classicists whose work she had once rejected. She also eagerly read works of history, science and philosophy with Mam'selle's enthusiastic encouragement. Above all she used her observation, noting how in the redevelopment of Paris many precious historic buildings were being sacrificed, that behind the façades of Haussmann's new boulevards and squares speculators were busy jerry-building. Slums even less picturesque than the original, which at least had character, were multiplying. To her developing social conscience it was a concept to benefit not the little people of Paris but the bourgeoisie of whom her mother was a prime example, a former demimondaine entirely compromised by success and possessions. She rebelled against it and developed a feeling for the under-privileged that was never to leave her. The old Duc and others among her mother's high-placed circle told Judith not to take Sarah seriously. She was performing, they said, the ritual duty of a new generation in being over-critical of its predecessors. Nevertheless, Sarah's compassion for the deprived would influence her throughout her life and in combination with a capacity to enjoy herself give her a certain sense of guilt in the acceptance of the fruits of success.

But she considered the plans for the new Paris Opera indisputably shameful. It was inspired by the eighteenth-century Bordeaux Opera which at the time of the port's heyday had catered to the tastes of rich merchants. Paris was to have an edifice to gratify the needs of even richer strata, who cared far more for fashionable occasions than for the arts. For example, a private carriage-way would lead to the entrance to the royal box, vast halls and grand stairways would enhance the glitter of receptions for French and foreign dignitaries, tiers of boxes would give privacy to wealth and rank or hide their amorous escapades, and the auditorium would be cluttered with decorative effects from every conceivable period. What had this to do with art? How could this provide a population hungry for education with wit and wisdom? Sarah believed that such enterprises were very ill-conceived and that the vast funds they absorbed would be better spent creating theatres for the people. It was not an outlook to find sympathy from the *sociétaires* at the Comédie-Française.

Nevertheless, she enjoyed every moment of that summer during which she was groomed to play there. She delighted in particular in the attentions of the Comédie's backstage staff: the hairdressers, make-up people, designers, seamstresses and set-makers, most of whom had been with the Comédie for years. They had seen fledglings before and were tolerant of their airs and graces. For many of the novices this season of anticipation would prove illusory. Safely married, their stage ambitions put away, this summer when it seemed the sun shone for them alone would be a memory, so why not gild it for them by playing up to their game of make-believe? So the workers in the theatre petted the novices and made them feel like stars. Besides, they were much more fun to work with than the older established players – like the overbearing Nathalie who came in late and treated them with imperious contempt. But Sarah was not an angel. She was demanding and sometimes impolite. On one occasion she was quite obnoxious with a stage-doorman whom she hit over the head with her parasol for quite innocently and affectionately addressing her as 'my little Bernhardt'. But these patient servants of the theatre, who had seen it all before, also sensed something unusual in her. No would-be actress had ever quite resembled her. This girl with the wild red hair put intuitively probing questions to them. Why was one make of rouge used in preference to another? Why did the new aniline dyes being used for the stage costumes produce more vivid hues than the older vegetable ones? Was this new silk from Afghanistan or Turkey? Had they seen Rachel play Phèdre? She charmed and exhausted them.

With the *sociétaires* she was less disarming. She could not forgive their unkindness to each other, their gossip and jealousies and their frequent use of coarse language. On looking back she realized she was at odds from the start with the stuffiness of the Comédie. It was trance-like in its adherence to traditions she knew to be outmoded. She respected craftsmanship but she also loved innovation. But throughout its two-hundred-year history the Comédie had never really been a people's theatre as a state theatre should be. Rachel, a Jewess of central European origin, had flashed briefly across its stage and given it a short period of true popularity with the ordinary people. She was an unpolished gem who possessed instinctively the common touch. Even at the peak of her career she could commit serious grammatical errors on stage, but she put new life into the old tragedies and had the public at her feet. Much earlier Bonaparte had used the theatre as an extension of his propaganda machine, directing the acting profession to reflect his triumphs in productions of the classics more grandiose than they were intellectually revealing. Now Napoleon III's Second Empire had set the scene for a return to those bad old ways, sustaining the Comédie as a citadel of classic tradition, but a sombre and conservative one.

On occasions during that summer Sarah persuaded Mam'selle to accompany her to some of the boulevard theatres, like the Théâtre de la Porte-St-Martin, the Opéra-Comique and the Gaîté, and had found in their unabashed melodramas a vitality entirely lacking at the Comédie. She believed in the dignity of the classics and did not want them vulgarized but she sensed that they could be humanized, as indeed they were being at the other serious theatre, the Odéon, to which she had also paid visits. What a difference there was between the actors, as well as between the audiences of these two theatres, the Comédie and the Odéon. The solemn actors at the Comédie had reached the end of their efforts. What use was there in exerting themselves further? Their public, which consisted of old subscribers in the upper social bracket, did not ask much. They were satisfied with the respect paid to traditions and had no knowledge of contemporary writers eager to have their plays performed. But the newer Odéon was a more stimulating sanctuary. New insights into the classics, especially those gained from modern psychology, were being allowed to influence every aspect of their production. And why, Sarah asked herself, must tragedy always be serious? One should have the freedom to laugh in tragedy and cry in comedy. There should be no rules. Rules excluded originality. The classics were not classics when they were written. Time had made a religion of them, dulling them with a patina of reverence to the exclusion of naturalism and objectivity. Why should great verse be declaimed? It should be spoken with both insight and craftsmanship, but not in a manner so formal as to render it meaningless. Nevertheless, the young actress-to-be was human enough to feel awed and overjoyed one hot August day when she stood in the theatre's cool arcades off the Rue Dophot looking at posters announcing the imminent debut of Sarah Bernhardt.

CHAPTER 4

Sarah's debut was not auspicious. She was plunged into high tragedy in Racine's *Iphigénie* and she was not at all ready for it. What understanding she had for the play was lost in a ponderous production that lumbered from one set piece to another at the expense of the thrilling psychological implications of this rendering of the Agamemnon myth.

To be in step with the stylized manner of the other members of the cast she declaimed rather than spoke her lines, which made the speeches sound histrionic and absurd. She was word-perfect and moved fairly well but the general impression she gave was one of rawness; she had not mastered the technicalities of acting or learnt to communicate with an audience. The only critic to mention her was quite right – 'She carries herself well and pronounces with perfect diction' – but little more at the moment could be said of her.

Thierry had got into his head the notion that the Duc de Morny was interested more in the girl than in her theatrical aspirations, and treated his new recruit with some deference. He gave her a dressing-room on the top floor of a house the Comédie rented on the Rue de Richelieu, opposite the stage-door side of the theatre and connected to the theatre proper by a narrow covered bridge. If de Morny wanted to visit his protegée he could do so there with more privacy. But de Morny remained a loyal friend to Judith and made no such approach. His reputation belied this restraint for it was rumoured that he was something of a rake and that a former valet had stolen photographs of his many conquests and was blackmailing him with them.

Sarah herself was so virginally intent on establishing her career that at this period she was virtually sexless. Even the occasional glances from lustful young actors seemed not to register. Most of them decided that she was an upstart prig and soon lost interest but she found a friend in a young actor named Clovis who liked but did not desire her; he was not sexually interested in girls. He had a bright, humorous personality and, sensing that his company could be enjoyed ingenuously, Sarah warmed to him.

He was an orphan. They had in common remembrances of lonely childhoods. They also shared an unusually mature ability to see through the pomposities of life at the Comédie. Sometimes at rehearsals they dared not look at one another for fear of breaking into fits of giggling, especially when Madame Nathalie, static, regal, centre-stage, boomed forth lines from the Master in a voice fit to deafen. Clovis too found no rhyme nor reason in the mannered playing so sacredly adhered to by the *sociétaires* of the French state theatre. But for Clovis she believed she would not have got on stage at all for her debut performance. Immediately prior to it she experienced an alarming attack of *le trac.* Stage-fright froze her in the wings in atrophied terror. She was quite unable to make her entrance. It was Clovis who gave her the sharp firm push which impelled her on to the stage. But throughout the play she felt close to panic and after the final curtain fled along the covered way in a fever of shame.

Yet Thierry did not appear unduly worried; he had seen worse and as far as *le trac* was concerned young Bernhardt had the temperament for it. She would probably be victim to it throughout her career – if she were to have one. He would know that in good time. But her two subsequent performances – in comedies by Molière – did nothing to encourage him and he began to think he had been over-indulgent with the Duc. Still, it would be indiscreet to fire her so soon. De Morny, after all, was the Emperor's half-brother.

At home Judith was a model of forbearance. Sarah felt the sting of her every compliment. 'You were very charming,' she said after reading a review that accorded her daughter only guarded reservations: 'The man's a fool.' But the climax came with a review of one of the Molière plays by Francisque Sarcey, the most powerful critic in Paris, who wrote: 'She is a débutante and among the number presented to us it is only natural that some should be failures. The pitiful part is though that the comedians playing with her were not much better, and they are *sociétaires* of the Théâtre Français! All that they had more than their young comrade was a greater familiarity with the boards. They are precisely as Mlle Bernhardt may be in twenty years' time if she stays at the Comédie-Française.'

Exactly! Sarah could not have agreed with him more. She was the victim of a mummified institution, helpless in the hands of an entrenched theatrical establishment capable of crushing any emergent talent. Well, she didn't intend to let them do it to hers. She would make a stand. She *must* make a stand . . .

The company began rehearsals for Molière's *Tartuffe.* This marvellous play about a pious rascal who introduces himself into a neighbour's home, tries to seduce his wife and ruin the family, was one of her favourites. It is an attack upon religious hypocrisy. In the years since she had left the convent Sarah had become more realistic about religion. She would never forget Mother St Sophie and the nuns who had so lovingly cared for her but she had seen enough subsequently to realize that their love and charity had scant reflection in the materialism of everyday life and that the Church was worldly. It preached conservatively to a humanity that was greedy, gullible and weak. Frenchmen, caught up now in the industrial revolution, were as much a prey to the class-consciousness of the established church as they had been in Molière's day. Sarah had little time for it; she related now to the fraternity of talent, which was classless. She liked Molière's comedies for another important reason. Because they direct a clear light on man's foibles and vices they are a hair's breadth removed from tragedy. His characters are unsympathetic and the laughter they cause is the critical laughter of the intelligence. He was not a museum piece. He spoke across two hundred years to the present, damning as false the conventions and bourgeois respectabilities of her time as he had damned those of his own. Only the Comédie's stultifying productions could dull his sense of the absurd, robbing him of pace and wit by their stylized interpretations. And so she approached her role in *Tartuffe* with rebellion in her heart.

The stage depicted a Parisian drawing-room. At the centre of it Madame Nathalie disgorged her lines in a typically formalized fashion. 'Don't fight him or make nasty *quarrels*,' she thundered in defence of the rascally usurper, '*Tartuffe* is here to *guard* your morals.'

Sarah, waiting in the wings to make her entrance as the maid Dorine, knew the emphasis to be terribly wrong.

Nathalie continued: 'I speak but the truth when I say all will be *grand*, if everything is done to *his* pious command.' The actress swept the air with a weighty arm. Those gestures, thought Sarah, are ridiculous. Finding it unbearable she began mimicking the performance, much to the enjoyment of Clovis beside her. Absorbed in this activity she missed her cue. Nathalie waited, then turned to catch the final seconds of Sarah's impersonation. From the prompter's box Thierry saw his principal's eyes blaze. He intercepted trouble by calling Sarah's attention to her cue. Sarah entered buoyantly. She gave her lines a light and saucy impertinence. 'In her imagination . . .' she slyly indicated Nathalie, 'the man is a saint but if she really knew him I believe she would faint.' It is almost a throw-away line and Sarah properly treated it as one. 'No,' boomed Nathalie. 'On that line Dorine takes three steps forward, bends over, holds her hand to her mouth and says thusly . . .' With one hand cupped to her mouth she showed Sarah how it should be done. It was a grotesque demonstration of an aside with all the subtlety of a cannonade.

Furious, Sarah gave a clockwork imitation. It sounded and looked ridiculous. 'Mlle Bernhardt, are you mocking me?' Nathalie asked.

Sarah looked surprised. 'No, Mme Nathalie.' She appealed to Thierry: 'But couldn't Dorine *not* take three steps forward, *not* bend over, *not* hold her hand to her mouth and just say the lines with a more natural confidence to the audience?' she asked.

Thierry hesitated. Nathalie answered for him. 'That is not the way Molière wished it!'

Sarah threw caution to the wind. 'How do you know?' she asked. 'Were you rehearsed by him personally?'

The actress faced her squarely. 'Molière has been dead two hundred years,' she roared indignantly.

Sarah paused. 'I know,' she said quietly. 'And so perhaps has this company.'

'Monsieur Thierry,' raged Nathalie, 'are we going to have a rehearsal?' Thierry put the question to Sarah. 'Are we?' he asked wearily. 'Then begin.'

That night Sarah's mind retraced the whole altercation with Nathalie. It wasn't a victory, she decided, but it was a good beginning . . .

But in challenging Madame Nathalie Sarah had crossed swords with a powerful member of the establishment. It was a folly she was to compound during the annual rite known as *la Cérémonie.* This took place on each anniversary of Molière's birth, 15 January, and was a pageant in homage to him. A bust of the Master stood on a plinth centre stage and the entire company assembled in front of it. Each player wore the costume of a Molière character and one by one was expected to declaim some lines, bow to the bust and lay flowers at the base of the plinth.

Sarah's first appearance at this ritual clearly had been stage-managed by the devil. She found herself ahead of the other ingénues in the line of players and directly behind Madame Nathalie who, carrying a huge bouquet of roses, wore a voluminous gown of funereal purple which had a sweeping train.

Thierry began the oration: 'Dear Master, the members of your company come before you to pay homage to your genius, your wit, your poetry. We bring our floral offerings, and with them our deepest gratitude for the illumination of your mind.'

At this point Nathalie prepared to make her obeisance. But pulling at the train of her dress to adjust it she found it would not move. Sarah had both feet on it. Nathalie tugged, but Sarah's eyes were on Thierry. So the powerful actress resorted to a mighty shove which sent Sarah reeling over to a stucco pillar on which she hit her head.

'Please accept, dear Master,' Thierry continued reverently, 'our humble tribute . . .' But why hadn't Nathalie come forward? He looked at the line of actors. What was going on? An affray had developed. Sarah, having recovered, was now deliberately standing on Nathalie's train and refusing to move. The two women were locked in battle, the younger's agility proving more effective than the elder's bulk. Finally an almighty thrust sent Nathalie plunging to the plinth. On the way she felled several actors and landed on top of a heap of them where she now lay like a spent avalanche. 'Good God!' said Thierry, and the curtain made a fast descent.

Thierry called Sarah to his office the following morning. Without exception every newspaper had revelled in the previous evening's fracas at the House of Molière. Nothing like it had ever before happened. An unknown beginner had assaulted a *sociétaire*, the most august of the *sociétaires*, in full view of the audience. They were gleeful for neither the Comèdie nor Madame Nathalie were much loved by the Press. One cartoonist showed the crushed hulk of Madame Nathalie strewn with roses and triumphant above it a slip of a mop-haired girl. The caption read, 'A Great Oak Toppled!' But Thierry's outrage was mingled with the knowledge that outside the theatre unprecedently large crowds were gathering. They wanted seats for any future play in which young Bernhardt was to appear. He couldn't remember ever having seen ordinary members of the public standing in line for seats at the Comédie. As he waited for Sarah he decided to berate her for what she had done and ask for her resignation. Then he would relent and graciously permit her to continue as a member of the company.

When she arrived he showed her the cartoon. 'We are not running a circus, Mademoiselle Bernhardt,' he said. 'Nor do we thrive on the notoriety of our minor players. If you wish to remain in the company you must apologize to Madame Nathalie.'

'Why?' asked Sarah blandly. 'I didn't stand on her train on purpose.'

'No?' Thierry doubted the truth of this.

'No,' Sarah said firmly. But she went on to say more quietly, 'Not for the first time. But after she pushed me I was livid with rage.' She leant forward to show him the bruise on her head. 'Look! It is Nathalie who should apologize.'

'She certainly will not do that,' said Thierry.

'That is her prerogative. And mine too.'

The girl was hard to handle.

'Mademoiselle Bernhardt,' said Thierry, 'you must apologize or consider your association with us at an end.'

But Sarah too had seen the newspapers. Whatever were the rights and wrongs of what had happened one fact was undeniable. The Press had taken notice of her. When they ignored her she had felt depressed. Now she was elated. Such notoriety could lead to a better offer. She would not apologize.

'Well, then, Monsieur Thierry,' she told him, 'I'm afraid the Comédie is going to lose its principal attraction.'

After she had left Thierry felt curiously let down, disappointed. The Comédie needed spirited new blood. But the publicity had gone to her head, and that was a pity.

For some weeks Thierry did not return her contract, hoping that Sarah would reform. He even cast her in a future play, but before the first rehearsal his principal *sociétaire* confronted him. She held the trump card of an outraged diva. 'One of us will have to go,' said Nathalie. It was the inevitable ultimatum, and Thierry knew it had to be Sarah.

CHAPTER 5

'I want to die, I want to die.' In her bedroom Sarah repeated the sombre incantation over and over again to herself. If she concentrated every facet of her will surely she would be spirited away. It would be like falling asleep, freed from worldly compulsions and the necessity to succeed, and she would live again somewhere else a less painful life. But no amount of willing was having any effect. She just lay there in her coffin with her mind in a turmoil of self-doubt. Why hadn't Thierry asked her back? Where were the new offers she had expected? What was she to do now?

She had waited for four months and nothing had happened. She had been made wretched by her mother's inability to understand. In the wake of the Comédie fracas, what Sarah had called valuable publicity Judith had considered a scandal. She had been shocked by it. Nathalie had friends at Court, Judith pointed out, who could embarrass her sponsor, the Duc. Wasn't it enough that he had an ailing Emperor on his hands? Day by day they became increasingly edgy with one another. Sarah believed the only place she was safe from her mother's condemnations was her bedroom and so she spent hours there, whole days, reclining in her coffin, the victim of her own disappointment and guilt. She had thrown away the only career she had ever really wanted – and now she couldn't even will herself to die!

In past weeks her sense of failure had been so profound that on the few occasions when she and her mother were able to converse they talked of alternative means by which Sarah might find a satisfactory life. One scheme was for her to open a confectionery shop on the Boulevard des Italiens. There she would sell an original speciality of her own creation, the *bonbon nègre*, a black concoction of coffee-flavoured chocolate mixed with liquorice. They even went to see the shop, which had a little flat above it. Judith thought Sarah might set up home in it. Anything to get her out of the house! Another plan envisaged a trip to Spain where she would buy pottery and other craft work for resale in a boutique to be opened in the Rue Dophot. Despite the obvious initial cost of such schemes Judith warmed to them, saying she would request the help of one or another of her well-to-do friends. She actually did so only to discover that this or that plan had been allowed to lose its savour in a languor of neglect and finally discarded. Sarah would then retreat to her room and not be seen for days.

She was convinced that all Judith wanted was to be rid of her. Her mother would never understand that one thing only would make her truly happy – a second chance to act. But Judith did understand this and turned again to the Duc de Morny. When he dutifully called she took him to Sarah's room.

He had heard about Sarah's coffin but it was the first time he had actually seen her in it. He was not amused. Life to him was precious. Judith was quick to explain: 'She wouldn't leave me alone until I bought it for her.'

'I've never seen anything so morbid,' said the Duc.

'She wants to be the greatest actress in the world or she wants to die.' It sounded ridiculous and Judith was relieved when the Duc made light of it. 'It seems to me that the second alternative rules out the first,' he said dryly. 'Anyway, she can't just will herself to die.'

'You think not?' Judith remembered the episode of the bottle of ink, the attempt to leap from a bedroom window. 'It wouldn't be the first time she's tried it. She has no thought for me at all!'

The Duc looked uneasy; he wanted a drink. 'I find this very depressing,' he said, 'and it isn't even mid-day.'

But Judith was at the end of her tether. 'What am I going to do?' she demanded. 'All she wants is to act and no one will engage her. Months and months and no one will take her on. I told her and told her! She should apologize to the Comédie. But no. She thought she knew better. Now she wants to die – as if that will prove anything!'

The Duc looked at Judith with compassion, then at Sarah lying in her coffin. Instead of being in this trance of self-obsession she should be out and about gaily flirting with youngsters of her own age. The girl was either very talented or quite mad. She might succeed in doing away with herself and what would that matter in the infinity of time? Judith mattered, however, for he believed she was the weaker. Sarah was probably very strong. Politics, so like the theatre in many ways, were also bedevilled by her kind of temperament. All Judith was asking was to be left alone, to be rid of a problem she couldn't handle, understanding very little of the complexities of a mind like Sarah's. He decided to try again. For Judith's sake he would try once more.

'You know, I might be able to help her,' he said. 'I have a friend who is the director of the Odéon. I might be able to persuade him to give her a chance. That is, if it's not too late.' He noticed that Judith's eyes were filled with tears. Sentimentally, he drew her to him. When they looked at the coffin again it was empty. Sarah, vibrant, was at her dressing-table as though getting ready for work.

But Montigny, the Odéon's director, did not want to engage Sarah. At his theatre on the Left Bank he had built up a company of young players that presented the classics in spirited new productions. The accent was on youth and equality. There was no room for temperament. 'I would dearly like to help,' he told de Morny, 'but her reputation has preceded her.'

'Just high spirits,' said the Duc. 'I know the girl well – as a friend of the family. I consider myself a good judge of talent.'

'Of acting talent?'

De Morny smiled. 'Look here, Montigny . . . have you seen the girl? She's waiting outside. Shall I bring her in?'

'She's disruptive.'

'Not at all. She's artistic, imaginative.'

'And crazy.'

'Surely that could be an advantage in a boulevard theatre like yours,' the Duc said. 'Or do you want to become as stuffy as the Comédie?'

He had won his point. Montigny, a former actor who once had been with the Comédie, knew how oppressive it was to young talent. He too had rebelled. At the Odéon he had succeeded in doing what Thierry had failed to do at the Comédie. He had attracted the man in the street to the classics; his was a true people's theatre. He crossed to the door and asked Sarah to come in. Before speaking he studied her. Then he said: 'Your hair is a mess, your nose is all wrong and you have the resistible appeal of a bean-pole.' She didn't flinch. 'Do you think you can behave in this theatre?'

'Yes, Monsieur.'

'We work.'

'So do I.'

'All right.'

There was to be a special performance for the Emperor. It would take the form of a poetry recital. During the evening she would be required to recite a few stanzas from Verlaine. It would be an important little showcase for her and redeem her in the eyes of the establishment.

'I'll do it beautifully,' said Sarah, but Montigny clipped her wings. 'When I think it's time for you to be self-confident,' he said, 'I'll let you know.'

When they had left, Montigny continued to think about

Sarah. She spelled trouble. He was absolutely sure of that, but the thought did not disturb him. He believed she had a talent and could be disciplined.

Trouble came sooner than even Montigny expected. Instead of preparing the verses from Verlaine as directed for her part in the recital, Sarah took it upon herself to select something different. She rehearsed the Verlaine to herself and decided it did not suit her. She chose instead a poem by Victor Hugo, 'Oceans of Night', a lament about sailors drowning at sea. She believed it gave her better opportunities to display her vocal attributes. What she did not take into account was the effect of even the mention of Hugo's name at the Court of Louis-Napoleon and Eugénie. To recite him in their presence would amount to a studied insult. He was a highly controversial figure living in exile on the British island of Guernsey off the Normandy coast. From there he was conducting a vituperative propaganda campaign against Napoleon III, flaying his imperialist policies. Already under attack from the Liberals for his disastrous involvements in Mexico, Syria and Cochin-China and criticized by progressives for such aggressions, Napoleon was a vulnerable target for press ridicule. He certainly did not anticipate that during a soirée in his palace an unknown young woman would speak verses by the hero of the Left Bank, a writer who vilified him daily. And so when Sarah, looking uncannily like a symbol of the soul of France, began reciting Hugo, Napoleon and Eugénie walked out!

Once again Sarah made headlines. 'The Demon of the Comédie Strikes Again' was typically sensational. Some journals carried cartoons depicting the scene. From most of the accounts Sarah emerged favourably for the Press generally was opposed to Napoleon and his extravagant Court. She was certainly not put out of favour with the mass public. The Odéon drew its audiences from Liberal, anti-Establishment elements whose numbers were growing as France's difficulties multiplied. They included the student community. To them Sarah had overnight become the darling of the Left Bank.

So Montigny wisely did not dismiss her. To have done so could have caused a student riot at the next performance. Besides, he was a showman and his instinct told him to present her to the public again – without delay. In pursuance of this he substituted her for another actress as the maid in the play to be presented the following night, *The Italian Straw Hat.* This farcical piece relies on quick entrances and exits, much business with props, and great pace.

Sarah was unbelievably bad in it. Not only did she suffer her usual stage-fright, she was perilously under-rehearsed. The result, despite help from Marie Colombier, the actress with whom she shared a dressing-room, was that she missed cues, fluffed lines, exited by wrong doors, and in one instance presented the all-important straw hat to the wrong actor! But she kept going to the final curtain. The audience treated her as a clown, delighting in her ineptitudes. At the end of it she felt depressed, defeated, suicidal. What was more, she knew that Judith had made a rare visit to see her perform.

'You were perfectly ridiculous,' was Judith's blunt verdict when she came to the dressing-room. Marie had already left it with a trio of young admirers. 'I was ashamed of you,' Judith added. Sarah watched her leave, haughty, presumably revenged for the insult of the previous night to her beloved Emperor. Then she was alone. Once again her mind seized upon the idea of ending things. Unable to resist a dramatic touch she scrawled 'Farewell' in greasepaint on her make-up mirror. Then she climbed on to the window ledge and jumped, only to land a few feet below quite unhurt. The dressing-room was in the basement.

'What on earth are you doing?' The voice was from inside the room. Looking in, she recognized her visitor.

He had spoken to her the previous evening at the Palace of the Tuileries. When everyone was berating her amid the uproar following the Emperor's departure he alone had said a friendly word. Montigny later had introduced them. He was Prince Henri de Ligne. 'I was trying to kill myself,' she said meekly, embarrassed to be seen by him now.

'From a basement window?' Because he was laughing she wanted to escape all the more. 'I'd forgotten,' she said. Then she bolted, running impulsively from the little courtyard down an alley that led to the street. He called to her but she kept on running. 'This time I must do it,' she told herself. It had become an obligation. She ran until she reached the river, climbed the stone balustrade of a bridge and began to lose her balance. As she teetered on the edge of the balustrade hands pulled her back. She struggled but the hands were firmly around her. 'Please, I'm serious. Let me go. I want to do it.' The hands tightened. 'The Seine is dirty and cold and you might hit your precious head on a rock,' Henri said. 'Then the Seine would be crimson with the blood of Sarah Bernhardt.' She still struggled, but more weakly. 'Don't laugh,' she pleaded. 'Please don't laugh. Didn't you hear the audience laughing tonight? Humiliating! I'm hopeless, ridiculous. I'm always thinking right and doing wrong. Even my mother despises me.'

'My mother thinks I'm ridiculous too.'

'You? Ridiculous? What had you done?' She was becoming calmer.

'I told her I wanted to be a farmer. I said I would make a bad job of being a prince. You see, I like animals and trees. I prefer them to people. I like growing things. Have you ever had a conversation with a tree?'

His small talk brought a smile. 'I like animals too,' she said. 'Animals and trees.'

'There are no trees in the Seine. Only fish. I have never talked to a fish.' His grip relaxed and she felt her own tension easing. Now the sight of the river scared her. She wanted him to go on talking and felt frightened at the thought that he might leave her alone by the river. Suddenly she asked with urgency, 'May I come with you?'

'Where?'

'Wherever you are going. Please take me with you.'

'But I leave for Belgium tomorrow. I am going home.'

'Then take me. Please. I need help. I want you to make me forget.' Slipping from his arms she climbed on to the parapet again.

'All right, Sarah, but please come down.'

She waited long enough to be sure of his concern, then climbed down. 'You frightened me,' he said, drawing her close. 'I'll take you home with me.'

They spent the night in his apartment on the Rue de Rivoli. They made love there. He was gentle with her and she felt no shame in submission. It was the healing she needed; she had never before felt so safe. Aware that she was a virgin he caressed her with skill and quiet authority; it was like a blessing. No one, not even her mother or Mam'selle, had ever touched her scars. He kissed them with cool reverence and it seemed to heal even those spiritual wounds. When he took her it was like a dying, but not the dark death of the Seine; it cleansed her of her inhibitions, of her regrets and fears, and when it was over she was a part of the living world again.

Henri de Ligne had come into Sarah's life just in time. Only a love affair could have saved her. Her mental anguish, her quest for success and self-esteem had all but burnt her out. Spiritual awareness had been no match for her consuming ambitions. She had little experience of human love up to now and what she had known had been woman-dominated. She had come to think of men as exploitative, as threats to her aim to be independent. What she had not realized was the power being loved would give her. When she knew that Henri was in love with her she set about renewing herself through him.

It was from the outset a one-sided love. Once she was restored to self-confidence she knew she could be emotionally independent of him. Although well cast in the role of prince charming, Henri was really the more vulnerable. If he were to fall in love with Sarah he would want to marry her. But his family, one of the most aristocratic in Belgium, would never consent to that. Once in love he was afraid of losing her and sensing this she felt the more secure. Henri really did not understand women. He thought them to be helpless; it was Sarah's apparent helplessness that drew her to him. And because he did not understand women he had no chance at all of fathoming a woman as unusual as Sarah.

Henri's country estate near Liège provided her with a setting in which to recharge. She spent many months there. They rode and picnicked and there were evenings by the fire. They made love with intensity. But the great house with its liveried servants and huge rooms got on her nerves, especially when Henri was away on periodic visits to his family. She became more restive as she grew stronger and knew that she would leave. Henri also sensed this. 'What is it that you love about the theatre?' he asked one evening. 'What does it mean to you?' She answered immediately: 'The chance to live a thousand lives. I find my only escape in it. I suppose it's the only security I will ever know.'

She chose a time when Henri was away to telegraph Mam'selle and on the same day began the journey back to Paris. Only to Mam'selle did she eventually confide the fact that she was going to have a child.

CHAPTER 6

Judith discovered that her daughter was pregnant a few months after Sarah's return to Paris. At first she lived in a tiny furnished room which Mam'selle found for her. Its whereabouts were kept secret but Mam'selle visited each day. As the time of the birth approached she resolved to find an apartment of her own. At no time did she consider a course other than that of keeping the child. No appeals were made to Henri or to her mother. Mam'selle's meagre resources helped to keep her going. This assistance came without censure for whatever moral reservations the older woman may have had were kept to herself. Both knew that as an unmarried mother Sarah would be sailing counter to every prevailing social wind, yet neither deflected from the practical steps that had to be taken. A small apartment in the Rue Auber was rented and to help equip it Sarah needed her personal belongings. She sent to her mother's house for them and on learning Sarah's address Judith paid her a visit.

Judith had heard nothing of Sarah for almost a year. No letters had been written from Belgium. But this lack of consideration she was willing to overlook providing Sarah realized just how concerned she had been for her welfare. In fact, it had been a period of rare quiet for Judith. 'You have wounded me,' she told her daughter. She looked with distaste at the almost bare room. 'I won't ask any questions nor criticize you for taking an apartment of your own, but you should have consulted me.' Judith was pleased with her own benevolence. 'Clearly you cannot support yourself. The only solution is to make a good marriage. The Duc and I have been discussing possible partners for you.' Her eyes alighted on an object beside the window. 'We feel that a good marriage . . .' Curiosity caused her words to tail away. 'What is that?' she asked.

'It is a bassinet, Mother. I am going to have a baby.'

Judith froze. 'But . . .'

'But I'm not married.' She was suddenly angry. 'What of it? That runs in the family doesn't it? I am a bastard too, remember.' Immediately she regretted this vehemence. 'I'm sorry.'

Judith summoned some dignity. 'Your father and I lived together for two years before you were conceived.'

'I said I am sorry. But I'm not sorry for being pregnant. I have enjoyed being cherished. I would do exactly the same again. For the first time in my life I feel free. The father knows nothing. If he did he might want to marry me.'

Judith looked old and tired. 'I will never understand you, Sarah. I think I had better go home.'

As she was leaving Sarah felt compassion for her; if there had been understanding she would have wept with love for her mother. But there was none. They were more than a generation apart. Judith had defied social ethics in her own day but wanted Sarah to keep in step with the very same conventions she had defied. So she let her mother go, visibly older, confused, an old lady with no more in her heart than vague regret that things were not different. A month later Sarah's child was born, a son whom she named Maurice.

From connections in Paris Henri heard about the birth of the child. He was still angry over the callousness of Sarah's departure. Yet he believed he loved her and he wanted to see the child. He found her walking with the baby in a pram in the Luxembourg Gardens. She was not prepared for the encounter. He asked her to marry him and she refused far too callously. She wanted to remain in Paris and work in the theatre. 'Surely the life I can offer is worth some sacrifice,' he said. 'As my wife you would be the Princess de Ligne with all the responsibility that implies. If I am willing to take the risk surely you too can make an effort to change. Acting is all very well in its place.' It was the most tactless approach he could have chosen to make. Her whole manner hardened. 'It's place is within me,' she said flatly, 'and I am not ashamed of it. You should make the sacrifice, Henri. I have played a princess before. Do you want me to give a repeat performance – in your stately home?'

It was unnecessarily wounding. In his anger he flared back at her. 'You have the mind of a vulgar whore,' he said.

'An illegitimate, half-Jewish *daughter* of a whore,' she reminded him, and there seemed nothing else to say. But Sarah hadn't finished. 'I told you I could not give up the theatre,' she said. 'I believe I have something to offer. When I marry it will be to someone who respects me for what I am. I don't want to change for your sake, Henri. Go back to your land. You are handsome, rich and not yet thirty, but I've met men of sixty with younger minds.' He left without further word.

Moments later an old organ-grinder touched Sarah's shoulder. He was holding a little monkey. 'It is yours,' he said. 'The gentleman hopes it will bring you luck.' She took the monkey and placed it tenderly in the pram beside her baby. 'It shall,' she said determinedly.

She left the Luxembourg Gardens set on putting Henri completely out of her mind. In view of her desperate situation that would not be difficult. She had to find work. Had she known that it was to be their last meeting, that she would never see him again, the parting might have been more painful. For later in her life when the struggle had been won she would look back upon the relationship nostalgically and with tinges of regret. She would recall it with deep romanticism, embellishing it with all the fertility of imagination Judith had used to depict the passion that had resulted in Sarah. Renunciation would be the recurrent theme – she had given up her prince for the sake of his family at the behest of his aged father. (Marguerite Gautier of *The Lady of the Camelias* was a role she would play three thousand times on the stage – and in her mind continually.)

For the present, however, the challenge of her circumstances was all-absorbing. She was running out of money and known to theatre managements not so much for her talent as for her ability to make headlines. With her small state pension Mam'selle heroically continued to contribute to running expenses. At the same time she acted as unpaid nanny and housekeeper while Sarah called at stage-doors and managers' offices, seldom getting beyond reception areas. On stylish notepaper bearing her motto '*Quand Même*' (for which the printer's bill had not been paid) she wrote to professional contacts. She had been touring abroad, she wrote, and had returned to Paris eager to show the public the new maturity of her talent. Nobody believed her. In the profession absence meant only one thing – she had been out of work.

Swallowing her pride she wrote to de Morny but the old Duc offered no further sponsorship. He was unwell, he said; affairs of state were absorbing his precious energy and France faced so many serious problems. This letter may have been shown to Judith as one from her followed swiftly upon it. Judith, surprisingly, offered the hospitality of her home and assistance in finding the baby 'a place at some suitable charitable institution'. The letter pointed out that by keeping the child Sarah was putting herself under a grave disadvantage if she wished to find a husband. For all its practicality Judith's letter concluded with statements that showed how much she had turned the matter over in her mind, and with what anguish. 'Society today provides no sustenance for the unmarried mother,' she wrote. 'I know that only too well. When I look back upon the struggle I had to provide for you, to assure you of an upbringing free from unnecessary deprivations, with so little help, I regret all the more that you will not depart from your obstinate purposes. Be realistic, I implore you. Perhaps, in years to come it will be different and a woman in your position will not be so disadvantaged. I cannot see that happening in my lifetime nor yours. All I know is that I would not wish to live my struggles over again. I beseech you not to so burden yourself.'

Unsolicited too was a letter she received from Aunt Rosine. In her old age this lady had become fanatically religious. Sarah received a sum of money sufficient to pay a week's rent, some evangelical literature and a weird, enfeebled scribble urging her to 'abandon a life of wickedness and offer herself to God'. This struck her as particularly specious because her own life had never been so dedicated. What was more she considered her aims quite godly – to work and to keep her child.

Nevertheless, despite Mam'selle's sacrifices Maurice was not getting all he needed, the flat remained partly furnished and her wardrobe was depleted and unfashionable, consisting as it did mainly of maternity clothes. Her chances of interesting managements were being further handicapped by a dowdy appearance. For all her sense of purpose, Sarah was not as well equipped as Judith had been in her time to deal with a similar situation. Life as a petted courtesan did not appeal to her and even if she had possessed the necessary qualities there were fewer opportunities to pursue it. The social climate had changed and the days of the great courtesans were numbered. Taking a lead from England, France was undergoing an industrial revolution which brought radical shifts in the class structure. There was a hunger for education among the working people. Women, at least psychologically, were preparing to emerge from bondage. The top men of industry were a breed very different from the rich of Judith's day. A courtesan of the old style enjoyed a certain independence but to be kept would have seemed to Sarah as restrictive as marriage, as defeating of her will to live by her talent. Men would not have found in her egotism, her intellectual drive, the flattering indulgence Judith had the personality to offer her patrons. Sarah was the new woman ahead of her time. The very thought of such compromises was dispiriting. She had to succeed on her terms – or disappear from the face of the earth.

When she looked at Maurice and saw in him a duplication of herself she vowed that he would not be deprived of a loving home background simply because society had not yet realized that she alone had the right to give him one. If there were a God her purposes would be seen as just. With this faith she persevered in her search for work but apart from the Comédie, where she thought an approach useless, only one possibility remained – would Montigny have her back?

The one theatre she had not approached was the Odéon. It was their company she most regretted leaving. It had continued to increase in popularity, especially with the younger people. Nine or ten different plays were being presented there every week, fifty or sixty over the entire season. It still played the classics but it had extended its repertoire to include the work of new playwrights. Its company was young and ambitious and it had come to be called The Theatre of Youth. When she looked back on her few months at the Comédie-Française, surrounded by stilted, gossipy, jealous people, and compared that with her lost chance at the Odéon she was filled with remorse. Yet, being Sarah, she found excuses for herself. Montigny, intent upon capitalizing on her notoriety, had put her into a play insufficiently rehearsed. The play had been a comedy and he should have had the vision to see that she was destined to shine brightest in tragic roles. She even persuaded herself that the Odéon owed it to her to give her another opportunity. This attitude strengthened as her position became increasingly desperate, debts mounted and the spectre of failure could no longer be ignored. Somehow she had to see Montigny.

The plan she devised was itself pure melodrama. It entailed dressing in the most threadbare of her clothes so as to look a picture of neediness. Thus attired she would sit in Montigny's outer office with her baby in her arms and wait there for as long as it took for him to see her. On the morning of her departure Mam'selle prevailed upon her not to take Maurice because the boy was not in the best of health. In substitute Sarah decided to take the monkey! So with the little animal wrapped in swaddling clothes she set off hoping to see Montigny.

She had been waiting at the Odéon for over an hour when someone came in from the street door. It wasn't Montigny but the up-and-coming playwright Victorien Sardou. They had met briefly before at the Odéon. This could be a lucky encounter for she knew that his play *The Black Pearl* was in preparation. Concerned to see her looking so pale and impoverished he spoke to her. 'I know your face,' he said.

'My name is Sarah Bernhardt,' she said.

'Are you here to see Montigny?'

'Yes, Monsieur. I need work.'

Sardou – tall, genially handsome, an eccentric sort himself – said he would see what he could do, and disappeared into Montigny's office. A little later she was invited in.

'This lady needs work,' said Sardou, but Montigny had immediate doubts.

'That may be,' he said. 'I remember Mlle Bernhardt well. She was one of my keenest disappointments. You see, I need actresses who condescend to be at the theatre on the second night too. What made you run away?'

'I understand, Monsieur,' said Sarah.

'I'm sure you do,' Montigny said somewhat cynically.

She knew she should take the initiative. 'You are quite right. I did run away on that first night. I ran from your theatre to kill myself. I very nearly jumped into the Seine.'

Montigny seemed ready to sympathize.

'But I won't hold that against you,' added Sarah.

Montigny was taken aback. 'You imply that I was responsible?'

'You gave me less time than I needed to prepare. I was very much under-rehearsed. And the play didn't suit me.'

'I humbly apologize,' Montigny said dryly.

'I accept your apology,' said Sarah, 'but I want you to know that I have learned much about life since then. This experience I can use on the stage. I know that if you can find me something in Monsieur Sardou's play I will prove to you just how much I have changed. Melodrama, in any case, is far more suited to me.' She decided to pull out all the stops. 'Oh, gentlemen, I beg you. Acting is all I can do, the only way my baby and I can eat.' Her voice rang with anguish and mounted to a climax with a sonorous entreaty: 'I appeal to you, I beseech you, if I can't work for you we'll . . .'

'Stop, Mlle Bernhardt,' Montigny cried. 'I will find you something.' But Sarah was wrapped up in her performance. She was about to collapse.

'The baby!' cried Sardou. 'You will drop the baby!'

Montigny rushed forward. In grabbing the endangered bundle he removed the swaddling clothes. Out jumped the monkey!

'Good God!' he said in stupefaction. 'Is nothing sacred?'

CHAPTER 7

Chastened by the months of unemployment Sarah rejoined the Odéon company. She was thrilled to be working again. Montigny gratefully noted that she was more amiable in her relationship with the company, punctual at rehearsals, always word perfect and that she never missed a performance. Deciding that she could continue with the company, he began casting her in various roles some of which were very diminutive, not much more than walk-ons, for he believed she still needed lessons in humility. The range of the plays covered everything from tragedy to comedy, the classics to works by moderns, because he wanted her to develop technically.

Sardou had been more pleased than Montigny with her performance in *The Black Pearl* but Montigny was satisfied with her new professionalism. Sarah was happy. She had begun to live for the stage. Life at the Odéon was unremitting toil but she loved it. She would awake at nine and study her lines while still in bed. Then there were morning and afternoon rehearsals for plays other than the one to be given that night. During some weeks she would appear in as many as three different plays while also learning parts in three more. Responsibility for Maurice encouraged self-discipline but she actually gave little time to him. Mam'selle was in charge. What really drove her was a feeling of commitment to the theatre; at last she was being true to her vocation.

Montigny still thought her legs too thin, her hair nightmarish, but he admired the quality of her voice. It became richer in tone as her stage confidence grew and it was already being talked about by playgoers. Impressed by her desire to work and her capacity for it, he urged her above all to concentrate on technique. Fine acting, like any other art, was not wholly a gift from the gods; it had to be nurtured with technique. Matters such as presence, projection, memory should be her vital concerns. An actor could become great overnight but only after months, more usually years, of mastering the techniques of the craft.

Sarah listened, worked, waited. She knew that notwithstanding Montigny's reserved opinion of her she was learning technique very rapidly. What she wanted was a role which would allow her to prove it. But he seemed deliberately to cast her in roles that did not suit her, such as in comedy, plays by Marivaux for which she had no feeling. Into her mind crept the dismaying suspicion that her real talent was being ignored at the Odéon as once it had been at the Comédie.

However, during the next season he presented her with a wealth of roles in plays of Georges Sand, Shakespeare, Molière and Racine. Each time the role was more important and her ambition likewise grew. Eventually she was cast as Cordelia in *King Lear*, the opportunity she had longed for. She acquitted herself very well. It was the most controlled performance she had ever given. The golden voice displayed a sweetness and delicacy that had never been heard before and she expected high praise from Montigny. It was not forthcoming. But for Sardou, with whom she had become close friends, she would not have known his opinion. Sardou had spoken to him after the first performance and had praised Sarah but Montigny had replied grudgingly, 'She's good, but she's not yet great.' That was something. Being of a practical disposition she asked for an increase in salary – and got it. But the money was still meagre and afforded no luxuries. She was still unable to pay the indispensable Mam'selle a regular wage.

From Sardou she learnt a lot about theatrical craftsmanship. This urbane, attractive and witty man would in time become France's most successful popular playwright and a brilliant director too. Over the years critics would flay him for the superficiality of his work but acknowledge him as a supreme master of stage technique. Since *The Black Pearl*, not the best of his plays, he had followed Sarah's progress, coming often to the Odéon to watch her perform. After many a performance they would go out to supper together and talk theatre into the small hours. They found in each other's opposite natures the basis of a close and lasting friendship. With a perennial capacity to find humour in life he deflected her from an over-serious attitude to it. He mixed easily and made friends and through him she gathered a social circle of her own. This added to her feeling of well-being. When he asked her to go to bed with him she consented out of pleasure more than desire. She knew he was gregarious and that their affair would not last long. Her only fear was that it would endanger a valued friendship. But when it was over they both still sought each other's company and were overjoyed to realize that the friendship would continue. It was destined to last for forty years. In the course of it he would write some of her biggest successes and he would never lose his sense of wonder that this strangely vulnerable woman could on stage transform his transient and unprofound plays into works that seemed durable and inspired. And neither would ever realize that of the profusion he wrote the only play to be remembered by future generations would be *Tosca* – because Puccini turned it into an opera!

One member of the Odéon company Sarah regarded as a friend was the vivacious young actress Marie Colombier. They had first met when both were students at the Conservatoire. Marie's luscious beauty stirred the artist Manet, who painted a deliciously provocative portrait of her. Sarah even at her most feline could never match the obvious sensuous femininity with which Marie excited her fans. Sarah's appeal was more mystical. Because of this oppositeness of personality the two women got along well together. Sarah found Marie's rich extroversion and sometimes spiteful conversation an antidote to her own reticence and introspection. She rather envied her easy popularity with men. Marie admired Sarah's talent which she honestly admitted to be superior to her own. When performing in the same play with Marie she had no fear of being outshone, which for someone as ambitious as Sarah also helped their friendship along.

One night, after a performance of *King Lear*, Marie, who had been in the audience with her latest boy-friend, came to her dressing-room with him. She introduced the shy young poet François Coppée. He had established a unique reputation for himself with poems and short plays that dealt with the joys and sorrows of the little people of Paris. He had come to be known as the *poète des humbles*, a sort of troubadour of the working folk. Marie explained that François had just finished writing a verse play that she considered would ideally suit the two of them. Coppée nervously handed Sarah the slim manuscript which she took home to read that night. It was *Le Passant*, a love story set on a moonlit terrace in Renaissance Italy. It had only two characters, a spellbound idyll concerning a beautiful Florentine lady named Sylvia and a handsome boy troubadour named Zanetto. Sylvia's trouble is that she has a heart of stone, but the boy's innocent rapture on seeing her almost melts it, but not quite. He offers to be her minstrel slave and on being turned down takes up his lute and goes sadly on his way. That was all there was to this charming, inconsequential and improbable piece. Sarah was immediately in love with it. She saw at once what she could do with the role of Zanetto. It had never occurred to her to play a boy before but in relation to the abundant femininity of Sylvia it would be the most natural thing in the world. In the morning she took the script to Montigny and asked him to let her do it.

For weeks Montigny deliberated. Sarah continued to perform in plays in the repertoire to which had now been added *King Lear*. There could be no doubt that the packed houses on the nights she played Cordelia testified to the fact that she had become the Odéon's main attraction. Conscious of this she showed some signs of reversion to her former temperamentality. One evening before the curtain rose the call-boy found her stretched out on the floor of her dressing-room. She was white as a sheet and apparently lifeless. He rushed to Montigny and told him Mme Bernhardt had suffered a seizure and was probably dead. Montigny went to see for himself. There seemed little doubt about it – to all intents and purposes she appeared to have expired. Her body was quite inert. Dejectedly, he sent for a doctor although that seemed merely a formality. He then announced to a restive audience that the performance could not take place. Backstage, some of the cast and stagehands were weeping. But when the doctor arrived Sarah rose and amid laughter asked what they thought of her impersonation. Montigny flew on to the stage again to inform the audience, many of whom were already leaving, that there had been a misunderstanding. This apparently pointless prank infuriated Montigny but it made newspaper copy and increased Sarah's value as an attraction.

In addition to manufacturing publicity it came to her gratuitously. Her apartment caught fire. The news that her home was burning reached her while she was at the theatre. A cab rushed her to the Rue Auber where a crowd had gathered. Dense smoke poured from her front windows and the porch was ablaze. Even the firemen were hesitant to cross it. Although Sarah's terror of fire instilled by the experience at Quimperlé amounted to a neurosis, she knew that Maurice and Mam'selle were asleep in the building. She rushed round to the Boulevard Haussmann where there was a rear entrance to the flats, climbed up the servants' stairway and roused her son and Mam'selle. She wrapped

Maurice in a blanket and with the aid of a fireman's ladder got Mam'selle and the boy out of the building just in time.

The event made front-page news. But one columnist suggested that the publicity-seeking actress had started the blaze herself. Even more malicious was a columnist's suggestion that she had done it for the insurance money. Nothing could have been further from the truth. Sarah had actually forgotten to renew her insurance. The flat had been gutted, all its contents destroyed, but there was no hope of compensation. Every precious personal belonging, jewellery, letters, press clippings, her books, a portrait of her mother by the pastelist Severin, the old Dutch furniture from her room at Judith's house and a little money very arduously saved were ashes and rubble.

Sarah pined her losses in a mood of dejection for several days. But the fire had one happy consequence. It reunited Sarah with her mother. Judith for long had wanted to extend the hand of reconciliation, especially in the light of her daughter's progress. In the fire she found a godsent opportunity. She took into her home on the Rue St Honoré both Sarah and her four-year-old boy. They were to remain there until Sarah had enough money for a new flat of her own. A quainter outcome of the trauma was that Sarah decided that in future she would insist that theatre managers pay her not in cash but in gold coins. It was a somewhat femininely illogical reaction to the proof she had received of the insubstantiality of material assets – and the wisdom of paying insurance premiums.

That Sarah had become quite a celebrity was substantiated by the fact that following the fire she received letters of condolence and offers of help from members of the public. In addition, the manager of a fashionable hotel, aware of her publicity value, offered 'a suite of rooms on the first floor consisting of two bedrooms, a large drawing-room, a small boudoir and a bathroom, free of charge' –

if she would consent to dine there every evening for a month. In view of this a PS to his letter seemed somewhat stingy – 'You would only have to pay for fresh supplies of plants for your drawing-room.' The offer was declined. But it was the sympathy of total strangers that touched her. Some even sent gifts to replace her lost possessions. These included two tortoises in replacement of those from her menagerie which the Press reported had been destroyed in the fire. Other correspondents sent poems saluting her bravery.

Some letters were guardedly anonymous but a handwriting expert would easily have detected that the majority of them were written by women. For Sarah was emerging as a personality both admired and envied by them. That still unemancipated legion saw in her life-style their own unrealized aspirations and unrealizable dreams. In interviews she gave to the Press she never hid the fact that she was an unmarried mother; often she plainly stated her belief in equal rights for women. This charisma she developed for her own sex was of great significance to her. She felt it to be a responsibility. After she had played other male roles on the stage she began increasingly to challenge the discriminatory conventions. Aspects of her way of life were to suggest that *la différence* was less important than the quality of life and love. This uncompromising attitude backed by a moral courage so unusual in her time increased her interest to newspaper columnists, who never really understood her. Was she being controversial or eccentric when she commissioned Worth to design her a trouser-suit? The Press could never decide and Sarah would not help them. She said simply that trouser-suits were more comfortable than wasp waists or bustles.

When she talked to the Press as now she did quite frequentlly she spoke on other subjects besides the theatre: the enfranchisement and education of women, religion, bringing up children, politics, love, war were all within her scope. She was becoming a public personality – and a true original. At twenty-six she was that rarity in her time, a woman with the power and gift to express herself.

Yet she still had not shown that she was more than a capable actress with an aptitude for notoriety. The chance to do so came with the staging of *Le Passant.*

The role of the Renaissance page proved to be her first indisputable triumph. The technique that Montigny had looked for, that had seemed still unpolished in *King Lear*, was at last emphatically apparent. As the unsullied love-lorn youth she looked ethereal. She had designed the costume herself. She moved with such agile grace and spoke in such fresh, limpid tones that the poet Théophile Gautier wrote: 'It recalls the jewels of the Renaissance, so preciously, so delicately is it worked: it is only a dream, but an enchanting dream.'

The first-night audience sat enraptured. When finally the wandering troubadour set off again on life's journey, his heart weighed down by unconsummated idolatory ('I fear I take that endless road again . . . perhaps not far from here lies happiness. Your hand shall point the way . . .') the theatre was absolutely still, spellbound in a pity too deep for tears.

It was a miracle worked by an enchantress and as the curtain fell on the moonlit terrace with the city of Florence under the stars distantly outlined the silence continued for several minutes before giving way to thunderous applause. Bernhardt had truly arrived.

CHAPTER 8

Fashionable Paris, more usually seen at the Comédie, flocked to join the younger, less affluent audiences of the Odéon. Huge crowds gathered nightly at the stage door. The character of Zanetto as interpreted by Sarah became a cult. Figurines and chocolate-box designs, the Boy Troubadour hat, postcards and printed scarves, Toby jugs and model lutes testified to the fact that she had created more than a mere stage character – she had woven a popular myth. No longer merely the goddess of the Left Bank she was now the rage of Paris – and she soon let Montigny know that she was aware of the fact.

Choosing a moment in the wings between curtain calls she said pointedly: '*They* think I'm good. They love me.' Montigny was not moved. 'There is a difference between art and popularity,' he said. Sarah stood her ground: 'From now on I wish to be paid in gold coins.' Montigny laughed. 'I'll pay you in gold when you deserve it,' he said. That night she left the theatre in a mood of sullen resentment.

The success of her Zanetto restored Sarah's prestige in court circles. A performance of *Le Passant* was given at the Tuileries by royal request. The Emperor seemed not to recognize the polished actress as having been the slip of a girl who had recited the verse of his most literate enemy five years earlier. In any case, Napoleon III had more awful concerns. Hugo, in fact, had been offered a pardon but had chosen to remain in exile on his island off the coast of Normandy. From there he watched approvingly as storm clouds gathered above the masts of the Second Empire.

Since the recent death of the Duc de Morny, Sarah's erstwhile sponsor, Louis-Napoleon had lacked a restraining influence. Trusting no other adviser he had taken the helm himself with occasional help, if such it could be called, from the Empress. Between them they had managed to isolate France from her European neighbours. England had chosen to follow a policy of non-intervention in European affairs. France badly needed allies in the face of the Prussian threat. An attempt to boost French prestige with the Great Exhibition of Paris in 1867 had proved ephemeral. No amount of showmanship would diminish the perils of France's position. The fateful game of chess being played by Napoleon and Bismarck, a far more wily exponent, was nearing check-mate. Napoleon, 'the nephew of the little corporal' who had hoped in his later years to write a life of Julius Caesar, found himself beset by problems of daunting magnitude. He was also fatally ill.

Germany was emerging. In reacting to the threat the blundering Emperor offended Russia (by supporting the Polish revolt of 1863), England (by his campaigns to create a rival Empire) and Austria (by seeking alliances with Prussia and Italy against her). In a few years he alienated nearly every state of importance in Europe. Internally France was in difficulties too. A succession of poor harvests and an industrial recession had created mass unemployment. Then Bismarck clipped the wings of the Austrians and Prussia was clearly France's major rival. The panic was on. Frenchmen rallied to the Emperor's call for mobilization and in 1870 France would declare war against Prussia. She would be entirely devoid of allies and the results of this folly would be so catastrophic that the Emperor's subsequent ignominious death in England would seem of no consequence at all to future historians. But the Second Empire would glitter right up to its final act of suicide with Paris as its most hypnotic jewel.

It was in that year of Sarah's triumph in *Le Passant* the most beautiful and exciting city in Europe. Its sparkling and profligate social scene was blind to the omens of the coming eclipse. It provided a fertile decadence upon which art flourishes, and it was against this background that Sarah rose to fame.

There were theatres everywhere: the new L'Opéra on the Rue le Pélétier, the Opéra Comique, the Théâtre Italien, the Bouffes Parisiens, the Gymnase and others on and around the Grands Boulevards. There were sparkling salons known as dance-halls, the most famous of which was the Bal Mabille on the Allée des Veuves close to the Champs Elysées. Lavishly decorated with red damask and gilded mirrors it was lit by five thousand gas jets. Girls of every description and every price circulated within for custom and there were the can-can dancers to titillate the male appetite.

It was a city of noise and colour and crowds, especially in good weather when life was lived outdoors. Bands played in the squares, steam organs serenaded at street corners and seafood or wild strawberries were sold at sidewalk stalls. The fashionable cafés were the Café Riche, the Café de Paris, Voisin, Café Hardy and Brébant but romance flourished and poems were made at humbler cafés all over the teeming night city. For the very rich there were the Café Anglais and Maison Dorée on the Boulevard des Italiens with their private dining-rooms.

The age also saw the opening of the first department stores – Le Printemps, Au Bon Marché and Le Louvre. The House of Worth was at 7 Rue de la Paix. For foreign visitors there were hotels such as the Bristol on the Rue du Faubourg St Honoré, the Hotel du Louvre (where Mark Twain stayed during a visit to the Paris Exhibition) and the Grand opposite the Boulevard des Capucines which had no less than eight hundred rooms. They catered in particular for the all-powerful English on the Grand Tour.

Haussmann's ruthless restructuring of Paris under the Emperor's direction had created the most modern, the most exciting city in Europe with tree-lined boulevards and vast new parks. There was the Bois de Vincennes and the Parc Monçeau while the incomparable Bois de Boulogne now had the lakes and waterfalls, footpaths and wooded vales de Morny had looked forward to. They covered two thousand acres intersected by forty miles of bridle paths and carriage-ways. The ill-starred Emperor was a statesman of startling ineptitude but in his new Paris (which also featured a new system of drains to service and cleanse dwellings and thoroughfares and a network of gas mains to feed fifteen thousand newly installed gaslights), he bequeathed to France and to all mankind the loveliest of cities. One contemporary Englishman put it perfectly to Louis-Napoleon himself: 'You found Paris stinking and left it sweet.' For generations following the crash of his unreal empire, Paris would attract the young and the creative. The sounds of a Parisian spring, birdsong from chestnut trees, the laughter of youth along the quays would finally be his pleasant epitaph.

Young and purposeful and well on the road to fame, Sarah, in common with the actors and writers and painters of her own generation she was now meeting, felt a profound sense of unease. When she looked below the surface glitter of this city in the late 1860s, beyond the salons and cafés and gay life, the luxury and high fashion, the music and masked balls, the ugly reality was the widening gap between the rich and the poor. The majority of the citizens of Paris still lived in disillusion and squalor. The promise of affluence for all which the new industries had seemed capable of providing, a promise which the deluded Emperor also dreamed might be fulfilled, had proved a hollow one. Behind the brave new boulevards were disease-ridden slums where crime flourished. Police would not venture into them. On the perimeter suburban shanty towns gave mean shelter to thousands of families who had moved to Paris from the countryside. But the city of opportunity made no provision for housing the poor. Four-fifths of Paris lived in poverty.

Children died of neglect in the streets. Syphilis, alcoholism, tuberculosis, cholera were rampant. Child labour was exploitative. All this at a time when fortunes were being made by the new industrialists, executive salaries were princely and society entertained with ostentation.

Sarah was never a political being – she was too immersed in the theatre – but in spirit she allied herself with the realists and radicals. An establishment that disapproved of artists like Courbet and Manet was not for her. Had she been a writer she would have used her gifts as illuminatingly as did the Goncourt brothers. They were writing with clinical realism about the Paris behind the gaudy façade and clearly saw signs of the coming tumult. She made a friend of Zola who in hindsight was to describe the rotten core. But Sarah's art was too emotional to be of significance to contemporary problems. She offered an immediate experience and it was a life-enhancing one in a time of death-wish and doom. In due course she was to bring to the theatre a level of interpretation never before attained and express human aspirations more nobly than the materialistic pavilions of the Emperor's Great Exhibition had been able to do.

After the misfortune of the fire and during the period she lived at her mother's home Sarah saved what she could from her salary. She was helped financially by a windfall – a useful sum of money from her father's will. The Dutch lawyer she had disliked so much had managed to circumvent its clauses to obtain for the unmarried actress a sizeable slice of what had been intended as her dowry. It meant that she could afford a home of her own again.

She found a suitable apartment on the Rue de Rome and embarked on a buying spree, spending every penny on a wild assortment of furnishing and ornaments, some of which were expensive junk. The unerring taste in clothes that enabled her to be both a traditionalist and an innovator did not extend to the things she chose to live with. Her rooms came to resemble termini at which a miscellany of articles had been dumped. The salon of her new flat, a room much longer than it was wide and divided by an oval archway, contained hanging rugs and prints, diverse weapons and oriental heads which largely hid the wallpaper. The fireplace, huge and ornate, had on its carved marble mantelpiece a cluster of ornaments ranging from the exquisite to the dreadful, all huddled together on a cloth edged with silk braid. Elegant Louis XV chairs mingled with the tomb-like cabinets of the Second Empire. A cherry-coloured day-bed on a raised platform dominated the room. This extravagant divan was framed by a velvet canopy with tassels and red velvet curtains supported by Turkish spears. It was strewn with huge satin pillows. It was a lair to which she retreated panther-like for solace, sex or a Press interview.

Heavily pelmeted and luxuriously fringed curtains framed the windows of this remarkable room. The floors were strewn with a profusion of Turkish rugs, Persian prayer mats and animal skins. Bowls of pot-pourri, arrangements of exotic flowers such as tiger-lilies and numerous potted plants (some of which wilted in the hothouse heat she maintained in winter) filled the air with dank aromas that mingled with her own heavy perfumes and those from the scented cushions.

When she took up painting and sculpting as a concomitant to her theatrical career she made an adjoining room a studio which like her salon housed a mishmash of dubious works of art, finished and unfinished, pictures in rich golden frames (including a fetching one of Sarah by her friend Georges Clarin), exotic wall coverings and, towering above the polished wooden floor, a sculptor's dais upon which was mounted the work in progress.

The overall impression of Sarah's rooms was one of voracious energy, almost blinding colour and bohemian taste. She might have rifled the property rooms at several theatres and achieved a less bizarre effect. Yet it provided an appropriate background for her unpredictable changes of mood. These became more waspish and more productive of remorse as success, and the rigours of maintaining it, fed upon her nervous energy. Her tempers and tantrums were self-inflicted wounds, the dark side of a nature only genius could excuse. Yet in this improbable atmosphere Sarah brought up Maurice, under the saintly guidance of Madame Guérard, and kept a menagerie of animals including dogs, parrots, reptiles, a monkey and a quite untamable puma.

During the run of *Le Passant* Sarah's mother died, but they had finally become friends. Judith at the end came to terms with Sarah's individuality, took pride in her success, and had even begun to dote on her little grandchild.

This acquaintance with grief seemed further to harden Sarah's heart to the world when it didn't meet her demands. And her discontent smouldered and smouldered at every encounter with the implacable Montigny.

For all her success in *Le Passant* she still wanted to play high tragedy. It was her forte and she believed that with her Cordelia she had gone a long way to prove it. Montigny she felt wasn't thinking of her career – he was thinking of his box-office. He was content to keep her in *Le Passant* for as long as it made money. That was not good enough. Nor was his indifference to the fact that she was the theatre's main attraction. Instead of treating her as a star he continued in the pretence that she was expendable. What he didn't know was that she had her sights on a role that Rachel had played, the title role in Racine's *Phèdre*, the yardstick by which every leading tragedienne's talent was ultimately judged. Into this character she knew she could put her guts, her sex, her soul. Fatefully the chance to play it came when an actress in poor health refused the role. Montigny, anticipating the request, awarded the role to Sarah.

CHAPTER 9

The story of *Phèdre* is a Greek myth. The seventeenth-century playwright Jean Racine based his play on Euripides's telling of it in *Hippolytus* but he departed from the original and surpassed it in dramatic power. It is one of the great plays of the French language, a marvel of economy in writing with precise, beautiful couplets which impel the action forward at a thrilling pace. The role of Phèdre is among the most difficult of all to play because it imposes upon an actress the necessity to extract the compassion of an audience for a woman who through lack of self-control has destroyed a noble and innocent life.

Racine himself, acknowledging his debt to Euripides, said that for the main idea of the character he owed the Greek poet gratitude for 'the most lively portrait I have put on the stage'. He felt great compassion for her because she was 'neither entirely guilty nor entirely innocent'. She was driven by destiny into 'an illicit passion of which she was the first to feel horrified'.

Phèdre is the wife of the Greek island King, Theseus, and she is passionately in love with her stepson Hippolytus. The glowingly handsome youth is quite unaware of his stepmother's obsession and is himself in love with Aricia. This Athenian princess is his father's hostage with a rival claim to the kingdom so Hippolytus too believes that his love is doomed.

Theseus has been abroad so long on a warring adventure that it is generally feared he must be dead. When a report reaches the kingdom that in fact he has been killed the melancholy Phèdre, egged on by her companion Oenona, tells Hippolytus of her love for him. The youth is appalled.

The report of Theseus's death was false. He returns to find his wife suicidal and his son preparing to flee. Phèdre's miseries are now compounded with the fear that Hippolytus may tell everything to Theseus. But in the atmosphere of suspicion Theseus readily believes the lie Oenona tells him. Intent on protecting her mistress she says that Hippolytus has seduced Phèdre!

In deadly rage Theseus banishes his son but also calls on the sea-god Poseiden to destroy him. By the time the conscience-stricken Phèdre tells her husband the truth the youth has met an extremely gory death – and Phèdre kills herself.

Events so stark and torrid are the stuff of pretentious melodrama unless recounted with poetic genius. Even then they may be debased by mediocre interpretation. The actress playing Phèdre had to make of her a subject for human pity, for she can so easily be seen as satiated or merely ridiculous. Writing of Phèdre floundering in a love that ancient taboos pronounced so terrible, Racine says: 'She tries with all her might to conquer it. She prefers to die rather than to declare it. When at last she is driven to reveal it she speaks of it with shame.' Phèdre, in fact, was a victim of moral guilt inflicted by the heavy superstitions of the age. If that dark cloud of conscience is not convincingly conveyed then the play's grim portents can appear as too ponderous a commentary on the very human impulse to desire what is beautiful – as much ado about nothing.

To Sarah the interpretation of Phèdre seemed the ultimate challenge. All the great tragediennes had played it. Her art depended on marvellous articulation fuelled by mysterious inner fires; her Phèdre had to be the most revealing, the most convincing of them all. A great performance could make her the most respected actress in France. One less than great would diminish the prestige she had so far gained and she would henceforth be regarded as an actress who had shown much promise but had somehow just failed. She was given ten days to prepare.

When it was announced that she was to perform the role tickets for the first night quickly sold out. Many hundreds of people were turned away from the box-office. The opening would coincide with the anniversary of Racine's birth so the occasion would have an even more prestigious lustre. Because the role had been a great triumph of Rachel's every leading critic would be there to compare the two performances. All this served to increase the tension of these preparatory days. After long hours at the theatre she continued to study her role late into the night in the apartment at the Rue de Rome. As time went by she became quite unapproachable. Madame Guèrard, who was experienced at it, kept every distraction at bay. For Sarah was thinking herself into a character more complex even than herself, one as apt to exist on a knife-edge, whose childhood also had been deprived of true parental love, whose conflict was between passion and duty; between spiritual and physical fulfilment. For all its overtones of conscience, Phèdre's love for her stepson was a violent sexual passion, a lust for innocence. All this had to be conveyed.

At the theatre she was an example of discipline. But young Philippe, the actor playing Hippolytus, sensed that something was wrong. Sarah was far too inwardly excited for her own good. This talented youngster – fair, fresh-skinned and blue-eyed with the proportions of classical sculpture – had been chosen primarily for his looks but he had a good intelligence besides. When they rehearsed the scene in which Phèdre has to kneel in front of Hippolytus and beg for his sword (with which she proposes to immolate her love), Philippe found her submission unbearably sensual. He wanted to lift her up and take her in his arms, a reaction quite counter to what is called for in the play! Sarah seemed to sense this too. She was strongly attracted to the young actor. That was in keeping with her role but the attraction existed off-stage too.

As they were leaving the theatre on the evening prior to the first night she caught his eye and realized that he had been looking at her. Earlier in the day at rehearsals during the confessional scene both seemed to be deliberately repressing themselves. As a result neither of them gave of their best. Philippe still thought her over-tensed. He wanted to remind her that they were just actors. They were merely rehearsing a play. He would have liked to meet her away from the theatre, take her out and talk about things not connected with work. Preferably he would have liked to suggest going to his apartment where undoubtedly he would have made love to her. But she seemed unreachable and probably would have turned down his invitation to relax. It was a pity because he admired her and did not want her to fail.

Sarah was not herself any more. She had willed the character of Phèdre to impose itself upon her own so thoroughly that the long-suffering Madame Guérard was at her wits' end. She had seen similar transfigurations before but this time the extremity of it was beyond all reason. She wanted to tell Sarah quietly but firmly that nothing was worth so much anxiety, to remind her that she was young and that life offered many joys besides. But she knew Sarah would resent this and nothing would be achieved. So she resigned herself to the situation. But it came as no surprise when Sarah, committed to giving the performance of her life, told her at the last moment that she was in no state to go on. Stage-fright, that conditioned reflex she dreaded so much, had struck with debilitating force.

'I'm not going on – I can't,' she told Mam'selle. 'I'm very, very unwell.'

All afternoon Sarah had looked haggard and ill. Now, hollow-eyed, feverish, she paced up and down her dressing-room with the haunted look of the character she was supposed to play.

Madame Guérard said quietly: 'I know. I have already sent a message to Monsieur Montigny.'

There was a knock on the door.

'I can't see anyone,' said Sarah.

Montigny came in and stared at them both in disapproval.

'She's running a very high temperature,' said Mam'selle.

'I'm near *total collapse*!' said Sarah.

Montigny regarded her dispassionately. 'I don't care if you have to be carried on,' he said, 'you are giving a performance.' She did not react. His tone grew sterner still. 'Get on that stage or you'll never go on any stage again.' Then he turned his back and left.

For some time they sat in silence. Then Mam'selle said: 'It could kill you.' But Sarah had become quite calm. 'He wants a performance,' she said. 'I'll give him one.' But she looked terribly ill.

The call-boy came to tell them she had five minutes to reach the stage. Mam'selle watched her go behind a screen where there was a hand-basin. She heard her vomit, retching repeatedly. She got up to comfort her. Together they washed the basin clean. Sarah pressed Mam'selle's hand. She picked up a stage dagger and they walked slowly to the wings.

Mam'selle prayed that no one would speak to Sarah before she went on stage. With relief she saw that all the stagehands tactfully averted their eyes. Deeply enveloped in Phèdre's gloom Sarah listened for her cue. Hippolytus on stage with Oenone saw her coming – 'I'll steal away. My flight removes a hateful object from her sight' – and made his exit.

Oenone still on stage was joined by Sarah. 'Dearest Oenone, we'll go no further. I'll sit here. My emotions shake my breast, the sunlight throws black bars across my eyes. My knees give. If I fall, why should I rise? . . . Everything hurts me, drags me to my knees.'

Mam'selle sighed with gratitude – Sarah's agony was over. But Phèdre's had just begun.

As the play proceeded the audience became aware that something of profound importance was taking place. They were present at the birth of greatness. As Phèdre's anguish deepened so did their pity for her until it was as though the theatre existed only to shelter their compassion. When Phèdre laid the burden of her guilty love before Hippolytus it was almost unbearably moving.

'Listen to me, then. Let all my madness speak – I love you! Though you're my stepson, the child of my own husband, still I love you. Don't think I approve this passion which shakes my reason. More than you hate me, I hate myself. The gods have lit this flame within my soul. I cannot hide it.' Hippolytus wants to leave. 'No, don't turn from me. Have pity, Hippolytus. I love. I love.'

It was an extraordinary display of emotion. Near the end of the play Phèdre learns that her calumny has caused Hippolytus to die horribly. She takes poison. 'My eyes grow dark. I need never again see my deathly passion. I need never see a world without him.' She also stabs herself – and collapses as the curtain falls.

'My God!' cried Mam'selle, 'she actually has stabbed herself!'

Actors rushed to where she lay, but merely grazed she rose to take her curtain calls. For several she linked hands with Philippe. When finally the curtain fell she was still being applauded by her fellow actors and the stagehands. But Montigny did not applaud. As she passed him in the wings he took a purse from his pocket. He handed it to her. It contained gold coins.

In her dressing-room she told Mam'selle not to wait. She would leave when the stage-door crowd had gone. She wanted to be alone. For more than an hour she sat before her make-up table. Images and faces passed through her mind's eye – Judith, Henri, Mother St Sophie – and one by one they merged into a single longed-for face, unrecognizable, unknown.

She found the stage door quiet. Nobody still waited but then she saw Philippe. He asked if she would come home. She took his hand. 'No,' she replied, 'but you can come home with me.' They sat very close in the carriage. The night air revived her. When they reached her apartment they went directly to the drawing-room where a single light burned beside the divan. In the silence he began to undress her but she stopped him. Instead, she unfastened his clothes – until he stood before her the more naked. At the bedside she pulled him to her, knelt and pressed her face into his thighs. For a moment he let her remain there, then felt her tears. Tenderly he lifted her. 'You are no longer Phèdre,' he said. 'You are Sarah and I am Philippe.'

'Surely,' she sighed, 'it will be easier on the second night.'

They both laughed.

'It is going to be easy tonight,' he said and turned down the light.

CHAPTER 10

Sarah received notices of abject praise for her portrayal of Phèdre. Even the doyens who had seen Rachel bowed to this new mistress of the classical theatre. 'Not only her soul, her spirit and her physical charm but her sex were in the part,' wrote Jules Le Maître. 'Such bold acting would be shocking in anyone else. But nature, which has deprived her of so much flesh, has given her the looks of a chimeric princess so that her most audacious movements are changed by her light and spiritual grace into exquisiteness.'

Even Sarcy could go no better – 'This is nature itself served by a marvellous intelligence, by a soul of fire, by the most melodious voice that ever enchanted human ears. This woman plays with her heart and with her entrails.'

A veteran theatre-goer from England, Sir George Arthur, recalled 'a terrible mixture of triumph and self-loathing, a grief and horror of herself so poignant as to turn, for those of us who heard the agonized tones, horror for the sin into something like pity for the sinner'.

But while the critics raved Sarah had a simpler explanation for her triumph – 'the gods were there,' she said.

By the summer of 1870 Napoleon III, although personally inclined towards peace, was too ill to oppose the pressures for war which his own policies had largely created. Bismarck had out-manœuvred him diplomatically ever since the defeat of the Austrians by the Prussians at Sadowa. A victorious military campaign now seemed the only means of restoring French pride. The final humiliation came when Bismarck had brusquely rebuffed an important diplomatic envoy of Louis-Napoleon's and on news of this reaching Paris war fever gripped the city.

'To Berlin!' shouted the crowds on the boulevards, encouraged by the Minister of War's public boast that the French army would be 'across the Rhine in two weeks'.

The French government declared war against a well-armed, mobilized Prussia in precisely the way Bismarck had hoped for, labelling herself the aggressor in the eyes of the whole world. Moreover, he knew what the Paris crowds did not, that France's military forces were hopelessly ill-prepared. In any case, he regarded the war as 'an historical inevitability'.

On a day in July the Emperor, bent with pain from the illness of his prostate gland, waited on the railway station in the park of his summer palace at Saint-Cloud. With him was his fourteen-year-old son, the Crown Prince Eugène. The Empress was there to see them off. The royal train would arrive that evening at Metz in France's north-west corner where Louis-Napoleon would take command of a quarter of a million Frenchmen massing for an assault on the southern German states. And he would never see Paris again.

But on that lovely summer morning in July Sarah had every reason to be happy. Since her triumph in *Phèdre* she had developed into a consummate actress capable of alternating classic roles with sophisticated modern ones, some of them in plays by contemporary playwrights including Victorien Sardou who wrote with her in mind. She had played in Corneille's *Le Cid* and Shakespeare's *Romeo and Juliet* (in which she first played Juliet and later Romeo) as well as in Georges Sand's *Francis the Waif* and Alexander Dumas's *Kean*. Play-scripts reached her constantly and there had been offers from other managements hoping to tempt her away from the Odéon. Even the Comédie had invited her to return but she had remained loyal to the Odéon on an understanding with Montigny that she had the right to select her roles. Currently she was playing in *Fédora* by Victorien Sardou.

In her personal life she felt more secure than at any previous time. Maurice, now eight, was a likeable boy despite being a precocious one. He doted on his mother the more because he saw less of her as her public life became more demanding. And just as she had been pampered by her mother's smart admirers so Sarah's friends indulged her son. He took full advantage of it. Philippe, for example, was one of Maurice's heroes. If he had cause for complaint it was that no sooner had he become used to one young man in his mother's life than another took his place, though happily Philippe had proved more durable. Nevertheless, Maurice had the intelligence to realize that his mother was a special kind of woman. Actresses, Mam'selle had explained to him, lived differently from most boys' mothers and he was content with that. He thought her to be the most wonderful woman in the world. She was always getting her picture in the newspapers, which proved how wonderful she was. In fact, on that particular morning he was waiting for Mam'selle to arrive with the morning papers. There was certain to be something about her in one or another of them.

Sardou – his Uncle Vicky – was there. So was Monsieur Montigny. Best of all his friend Philippe had been with them all night because Maurice had peeked into his mother's bedroom and seen him. All was well with the world.

For Sarah too life was just as cloudless. But it wasn't in her nature to think about life when living it purposefully. On coming into her drawing-room that morning she might have considered how fortunate she was to find two men waiting for her, having just left another upstairs, but she did not. She had accepted a life-style which revolved around her. Montigny wanted to talk about the next production, Sardou about his new play. But first, she spoke to her son: 'Philippe will take you to play *boule* when he is ready,' she said. Then to Sardou: 'Where does the death scene come – at the end, I hope?' Then turning to Montigny: 'So many manuscripts – we're beginning to look like a printer's.'

It was bland, comfortable badinage but they understood one another. Three successful people and they were friends. The star, the playwright, the impresario. Later they would talk business more astutely. Not now on this beautiful summer morning.

'You'll have to decide, Sarah,' said Montigny. 'We want something to follow *Fédora*.'

'I've offered my new masterpiece but she hasn't even read it,' said Sardou.

'She'll have to choose,' said Montigny.

'She's too busy choosing lovers,' said Sardou.

Sarah listened good-naturedly. What a wonderful world was theirs. They were talented, celebrated, secure. All Paris knew of them.

'What is it, Mam'selle?' Sarah had seen her standing at the door.

Madame Guérard held a newspaper. 'I am sorry to tell you, Sarah, but our country is at war.'

It was not surprising – ever since Sadowa it had seemed inevitable – but it was none the less dispiriting. What made it worse was all the jingoism. The boulevard crowds were jubilant, but Sarah hated the idea of war. Although patriotic she was nevertheless an internationalist due to her mixed parentage, her feeling for art, her hope that one day she would visit other lands as an ambassadress of French drama.

'Will we win, Mama?' Before she could reply Sardou was telling her son that the French cavalry would cut through the Prussian lines 'like a knife through butter'.

Montigny was looking on the bright side too. 'After the initial shock,' he was saying, 'it will be good for the box-office. Men on leave need diversion, but nothing too weighty. The Comédie can be relied upon for that. We must concentrate on light entertainment. Now your new comedy, Sardou . . .'

She wanted to tell her son that in the end no one wins wars, that everyone is the loser, but Philippe came into the room and his interest in the subject faded in the prospect of a game of *boule.*

When Louis-Napoleon arrived at the frontier town of Metz he found it in chaos. French mobilization was in hopeless disorder. Troops were arriving by train at the central station without equipment and there was much drunkenness. Arms, tents, field kitchens, medical supplies, were in separate trains left at sidings on the outskirts. No organization was operating to connect the men and these supplies. Local barracks were totally inadequate. There was no money to pay them, no means to victual them. They wandered aimlessly about the city looking for food, drink and women. Every officer had been issued with a military map (it showed the German side of the frontier) but they could not immediately find their own units. 'Things here are not as far along as I had hoped,' wrote the Emperor to his Eugénie. Yet out of this confusion in five days some elements of the army formed themselves. A division launched an attack across the frontier and took the town of Saarbrücken. Four days later the grey steel of the Prussians threw them back. The entire French army retreated in disorder to Lorraine where they were pounded by the enemy's new long-range guns. Then the formidably mechanized Prussian, Saxon and Bavarian troops poured across the frontier in waves. What had started out as an invasion of Germany turned into an invasion of France.

That a new kind of military technology had outstripped them was now obvious to every French soldier but, understandably, not to the little boy prince who sent a telegram to his mother: 'I am very well and so is Papa. Everything is getting better and better.'

One French army a hundred thousand strong was entirely

surrounded at Metz and eventually taken captive there. The Emperor personally led another on a retreat to Chalons where most of his men gave up hope. Military police tried rounding them up from brothels and bars. But the will to fight had gone, especially among the officers. These swaggering Parisians were more used to ballrooms and colourful parades.

Dispirited and desperately ill, Napoleon by this time had lost all real authority. He was a forlorn figurehead obeying generals taking orders from Paris. Misguidedly, instead of being allowed to fall back to the defence of Paris they were told to relieve the army trapped at Metz. But the way to Metz was blocked so this second army deviated to the hill-enclosed town of Sedan. There, in what one French general later described as 'the bottom of a chamberpot', the Imperial French Army was cut to pieces.

Despite heroic French counter-charges the Prussian mincer ground the French to shreds in the blood-bath of Sedan. Five weeks after his departure from Saint-Cloud the French Emperor – 'passing blood and wearing facial make-up to hide his deathly pallor' – crossed the German lines and gave himself up.

When news of the surrender reached Paris mobs gathered at the Palais Bourbon, in the Place de la Concorde and outside the Tuileries. The Empress had assumed leadership of the tottering regime but there was no longer an Empire to lead. A Republic had already been proclaimed at the Hôtel de Ville. The mobs grew wilder. There were shouts of 'Vive la République' and 'Down with the Imperial family.' Eugènie began packing her jewels. By way of the Louvre she got out of the Tuileries and took refuge with an American dentist. He arranged transport to Deauville from where she sailed to England.

That night crowds moved along the boulevards hailing the birth of the new Republic. The dynastic 'N's' were chipped off the gates of the Tuileries. Imperial eagles were wrenched from the balustrades. Men and women danced drunk with joy unaware of the magnitude of the military defeat. Into the celebrating city Victor Hugo arrived after twenty years in exile to receive a delirious welcome. Patriotic zeal continued throughout the night. In the morning the newspapers began appearing. Then the crowds grew quiet. They dispersed into groups at street corners where they read that Prussian armies were advancing on the city. The Siege of Paris was about to begin.

CHAPTER 11

Montigny's prediction that war would stimulate entertainment was to prove utterly false. Paris was not to be a behind-the-lines pleasureland for soldiers on leave from the front, a refuge for the weary and the wounded. It was itself to be the front line. When the troops returned to it from the northern and eastern lines they came not as heroes to be fêted and indulged but as dejected refugees, confused and demoralized, to find the city in total shock. One consequence of this paralysis of fear was a Government order closing all the theatres. Sarah found herself out of work.

Just before the closure of the Odéon she was visited by a major attached to the War Department. On behalf of the Government he asked her to make a personal appearance at the front line – 'as one of the great entertainers of France'. To appear before the men 'in an open carriage' would boost morale, reassure them that life was proceeding normally in the capital city. Clearly the War Department was still unaware of the realities, that there was no stable front line. Touched by the honour she made arrangements to leave. Next day when only a few miles east of Paris they saw columns of troops ambling dejectedly towards them. They stopped the carriage and a sergeant spoke to them. 'It's not wise for you to go any further,' he said. 'It's become a rout, and it's very nearly over. We're the first of many. Please go back to Paris.' They turned the carriage round. They could hear in the distance the sound of long-range guns.

Philippe had been called to the colours. So had Victorien Sardou. But Sarah had no wish to seek new friends. The war depressed her. Paris was tense, xenophobic, jumpy, a seed-bed of rumour and fear. Particularly upsetting was a suggestion put about that she was of German origin. She refuted it with a public statement, but it stung and put her on her guard. She was worried about Maurice and decided to send him in Madame Guérard's charge to friends at Le Havre. It was a terrible wrench for without them the flat in the Rue de Rome was lifeless. But once assured that they had safely arrived she felt better and staunchly settled into her flat for the duration. But if only she could find something to do . . .

Troops were pouring into Paris from the north as well as from the east. There were bedraggled survivors from Sedan, cavalry regiments sorely depleted, infantrymen many of whom had thrown away their guns, and sailors and marines come from Brittany. A sizeable regular Paris garrison was bolstered by the paramilitary National Guard, hastily trained conscripts, and volunteers from the foreign fraternities: Poles, Britons, Americans among them. Eventually it could be estimated that a 100,000-strong fighting force had been assembled of uncertain capability and dubious cohesion but with a will to defend Paris. Their orders were to fight for every inch of the city, but the expected Prussian onrush did not come. Instead, the enemy began to encircle the city in a ring of steel. Once so consolidated Bismarck would be content for them to stay – for the time being – a tight cap on a bottle in which he expected the contents to putrify.

By the middle of September the last mail train had left the city, taking the line out to the west. The last remaining telegraph lines were cut soon afterwards and the bridges at Sèvres and Saint-Cloud blown up. From now onward the only means of leaving Paris would be by balloon. Mail would go by pigeon. Even so Paris resurrected a martial mood. There were parades and demonstrations. Hugo, as old men are apt to do, bellowed about the glories of the situation. 'To destroy Paris is to mutilate the world.' 'With Paris extinguished Europe will be in darkness.' 'Paris, which amused the world, is going to terrify it.' 'The world will see how well Paris can die.' Sarah found such perorations disheartening. She wanted to be useful, not to wait to be shot. Nevertheless the prodigious scale of the drama inspired her. A hundred thousand Frenchmen had been compelled to capitulate. The Emperor of France had handed his sword to the King of Prussia. Now German armies surrounded Paris. It was time to put into effect the spirit of her motto: *Quand même!* But how? What could an unemployed actress do?

After the departure of Madame Guérard and Maurice she sometimes sat in her apartment half dazed, missing the life around her, missing the affection. She found sleep difficult, suffered from nightmares. Then she read that some public buildings of importance had been put to new uses. The Gare d'Orléans, for example, was now a balloon factory. The Louvre had become an arsenal. The Gare de Lyon was a factory making cannons. Even the beloved Bois de Boulogne was a stockyard where a quarter of a million sheep and forty thousand oxen grazed, a living stockpile against the siege. An idea came to her. Why not convert the Odéon, now dark and lifeless, into a hospital for the wounded that were bound to result from the battles in defence of Paris? As a hospital the theatre would play its part in a drama far greater than any that had been performed there – the epic of Paris's fight for life.

She outlined her plan in a letter to a highly placed friend at the War Office. 'I hope you will listen to a young woman who, having known suffering, now wants to ease the suffering of others,' she wrote. 'I request a permit to instal an emergency hospital with thirty-two beds in the foyer and lobbies of the Odéon.' The plan was accepted.

Then she visited the Prefect of Police, whom she also knew, at the Tuileries, finding that so recently elegant palace had been converted to the drab purposes of bureaucracy. No footman came forward to open her carriage door as had happened when she played Zanetto there, gone was the faint perfume of elegant women from the great reception halls, and the Prefect's suite stank of tobacco smoke. Sarah used all her charm, for only from this important official would she obtain the necessary permits to equip and supply her hospital. He agreed to most of her requests but before leaving she asked him a further favour. In the cellars of the theatre, she told him, the government had seen fit to store gunpowder. Should Paris be shelled and the Odéon hit the place would be blown sky high! 'That is not the aim and object of a hospital,' she pointed out demurely. He promised its immediate removal. He was about to say farewell when she mentioned that she had yet one more request. He asked her what it was. 'That trench-coat hanging in the corner,' she said, 'would be useful to my wounded.' He handed her his coat.

It was November by the time Sarah got her field hospital working. Paris already shivered in what was to be the coldest winter in living memory. But a defiant spirit had beset the city. Morale was high and most especially among the working people. But they were dissatisfied with the strategy of the military government. The nearly two million citizens of Paris wanted action, not a passive policy of mere survival. That could only result in them being starved into submission. Stocks were being reduced week by week. When in due course the stockpiles in the Bois were so depleted that cats, dogs, rats and even animals from the zoo were added to the meagre rations the public began to demonstrate. They wanted the city's forces to take the offensive. The authorities they believed had a will to surrender. But the little people of Paris had their blood up and threatened to overthrow the provisional government should it deal in shame.

At last offensives aimed at breaking through the circle

of steel were launched. One by one they were repulsed at terrible cost.

For weeks on end Sarah's hospital, so modestly conceived, was deluged with the wounded and dying. To increase accommodation the auditorium was also converted. In the foyer and lobbies there were already three times the original number of beds and all the theatre's seats, the ornamental frescoes and the contents of the property room had been used to fuel the furnaces.

The hospital's supplies came from the military and were strictly utilitarian. To subsidize them Sarah twisted the arms of rich and influential admirers. From Meunier, the chocolate magnate, she obtained huge quantities of confectionery; from Félix Potin, the wealthy grocer, hundreds of tins of sardines. Through the Dutch Ambassador, who was a personal friend, she arranged for bales of linen to be brought surreptitiously through the Prussian lines. From Alphonse de Rothschild she cadged numerous cases of brandy and champagne. Apart from supervising she worked as a nurse after taking instruction in medical skills. With other volunteers she made tureens of soup and beakers of herbal teas over makeshift stoves. She helped stretcher-bearers bring in the wounded – and move out the dead. Unflinchingly, she ministered to soldiers in extremes of suffering, treated their so frequently gangrenous wounds. And she comforted the dying.

Only once did she come close to breaking point. A sailor hardly eighteen with the clean, honest features of Brittany was rushed in for an emergency amputation. He asked for her. 'Give him brandy – anything,' the doctor told Sarah. 'He won't survive.' The boy smiled at her. 'I saw you in *Phèdre* here,' he said. 'You were wonderful.'

She held him while the surgeon performed. The operation was too severe and the boy died. Sarah went to her old dressing-room and wept uncontrollably. But that night she went with some nuns to the defence posts on the city's eastern outskirts. In temperatures so cold that the Seine had frozen they handed out hot soup to soldiers in the entrenchments.

In time civilians needed help too from the hospital. The number of deaths from disease, cold and starvation was rising daily. From the foyer she sometimes watched women queueing for their unsubstantial food rations, pressing up close, blue with cold, stamping their feet to keep them from freezing. Frequently, a woman would be brought in from the cold in a state of collapse. To cope, more beds were installed. What had once been the green room, the refreshment room, Montigny's office became wards. Just before Christmas she received a letter through the Dutch Embassy from her son. He and Mam'selle were well. On Christmas Day, surrounded by helpers and the soldiers in their beds, she raised a glass in thanksgiving. Two days later the bombardment of Paris began.

At first the Prussians directed their shellfire at the clearly visible fortifications on the outskirts, but as evening came the bombardment intensified. Shells fell in residential areas, the brunt being borne by the more easily accessible Left Bank where the poorer people lived. Night after night the pattern was repeated. Because many of the men were at the perimeter defence posts casualties among women and children left at home were appalling. Pathetic processions of families pushing on hastily constructed handcarts personal belongings salvaged from blasted homes crossed the Seine bridges to the comparative safety of the Right Bank. Soon churches and hospitals became targets. Shells rained down on the Panthéon and the Church of Saint-Sulpice. The Church of St Geneviève was hit when packed with a congregation praying for the city's relief. Hospitals flew the Red Cross flag but instead of affording them protection it was used by the Prussians to sight their cannons. Shells fell on the Pitié Hospital for Children, the Necker Hospital for the Blind, the Salpêtrière Asylum for the Elderly, the

Val-de-Grâce Military Hospital and on Sarah's makeshift hospital at the Odéon.

By the sixteenth week of the siege the Odéon roof was so badly damaged that she moved her patients into the cellars. There conditions became steadily untenable due to the cold and danger from ravenous rats. For all her fortitude and courage Sarah had to give up. Patients were moved to the Val-de-Grâce. Some of them were to die under bombardment there. But for twenty she believed she could save she found a rambling flat in the Rue de Provence, close to the house where she had spent some of the loneliest moments of her childhood. This she equipped with beds and carried on until Paris itself fell.

It was not the shelling that defeated them but exhaustion, starvation, disease. Brute force had been unleashed against the civilians of a modern city, a war of trenches in public parks, of shells bursting on restaurants, of shell-holes on bus routes, a new kind of war but one that was to be repeated in other great European cities in the century to come.

In the nineteenth week Prussian guns were shelling the Invalides and close to the Luxembourg. It was a night of bright stars and a full moon. Sarah sat with her men in the flat in the Rue de Provence and knew from the glow in the sky that Paris was burning. Two days later the city capitulated.

The Siege of Paris was over but the ordeal of her people was not. Tragically, some of the most savage pages of French history were about to be written. Parisians had believed in the rightfulness of their resistance. Shared dangers and privations had given them a sense of community. They had behaved heroically. Surrender by the military, justified though it was by the situation's gravity, nevertheless seemed like a betrayal.

Sarah felt this sense of futility too. She had ministered to the dying, talked with women in the food queues. They had believed that their fortitude was in the cause of better things to come. She also knew that not all Paris had starved. The rich had been able to buy immunity from the shortages and the cold throughout. It had been from the privileged that Sarah had obtained extra supplies for her needy. When bread had been at its most scarce – black bread made of bran, vermicelli and starch – there were still shops in the high-class sections offering more nutritious bread at inflated prices. Yet the common people had tolerated these insolent displays, accepted rationing and endured the suffering with heroism and humour as their contribution to *la gloire* of France. But when their leaders surrendered it seemed they had suffered for nothing – and the anger of Paris at last erupted.

All through the siege there had been rumours that French armies beyond Paris were coming. The people had never lost hope. They had seized upon every optimistic rumour. Because of the sub-zero temperatures the pigeon post had virtually failed and the Prussians had shot down several passenger balloons. An attempt to get messages in and out of Paris in metal spheres fitted with fins by way of the Seine had also proved unsuccessful. The city became a newsless vacuum into which when the shelling ceased were injected the shameful terms of surrender. Bismarck had exacted from Paris – 'such a fine rich lady' – a crippling indemnity, the guarantee of a ceremonial entry into Paris and the right to parade the Prussian colours at the Arc de Triomphe. From France as a whole he would take the provinces of Alsace and Lorraine.

When Sarah read the official announcement she wrote in her diary: 'The light has gone out. What have we suffered for? Was it so that men of authority might play their power games? Women of the world – war is infamous! Men of the world – war is infamous! In the name of our wombs which bore you, of our breasts which suckled you, in the name of every woman's pain in childbirth let the hatred cease. Let Paris be herself again.'

But before she could be herself again, if indeed she could ever be, Paris had a terrible fate in store. A National Assembly, which had been sitting in Bordeaux while Paris bled and starved, moved into the capital intent on restoring old class structures. It passed a law that all debts and rents (nullified for the duration of the siege) had to be paid within forty-eight hours, suppressed newspapers and announced its intention of restoring the monarchy. Paris would have none of it.

In the middle of March revolution flared up, the Government fled to Versailles and the Commune of Paris was proclaimed. This citizens' government lasted into May. A second siege, this time by Versailles government forces, finally broke the will of Paris. The Versailles troops entered the city for a week of unprecedented carnage. Twenty thousand Parisians were massacred, Commune leaders were murdered, the city put to the torch. Haussmann's boulevards became gutted hulks. Even the Tuileries was burned.

A forlorn, exhausted stillness settled over the city. On a morning when smoke still hung in the air Sarah found her way back to her apartment on the Rue de Rome. It had escaped destruction but the shutters and windows were damaged. Inside, ornaments had been overturned, pictures were in disarray, and everything was smeared in an oily dust. It seemed the logical postscript to a year of madness.

What prospects now of a new beginning? The suffering she had seen made it difficult to believe in a theatrical career. She wanted to forget. Finding no other refuge more habitable than her rosewood coffin she retired to that. While she lay there she heard voices on the stairs – and she knew that her son and Mam'selle had come home.

CHAPTER 12

In the autumn of 1871 the theatres began to open along the war-torn boulevards. It was one of many signs of the city's will to live again. Gangs of workmen began clearing away the rubble. There was a frenzy of repairing and house-painting before the winter set in. By November the postal service was back to normal, the omnibuses ran on time and shop windows were bright with new displays.

No people were to display human resilience more remarkably than the French in the years to come. By 1873 the whole of the huge indemnity the Prussians had imposed would be paid and the last German soldier have left French soil. By 1878 Paris would be a glittering city and stage a World's Fair of a magnificence to dim memories of the old.

But in the weeks following her return to the Rue de Rome, Sarah could not believe in a hopeful future. Essentially a tragic actress she questioned whether a public that had suffered so much would want to be reminded of life's sadder sides. There were grim faces among the Parisians who daily made their way over the ashes and fallen masonry. Many women were in mourning. It would be unwise to attempt the heights again. But not wanting to infect her son and Madame Guérard with her gloom she took to sculpting. She spent hours in her studio, at first working abstractly with no idea of what would take shape, hoping to be guided towards a sense of purpose. As she continued she realized that she was depicting a face. But it began to look like the face of the Breton sailor who had died in her arms. She abandoned it and, turning to work with brushes and oils, using a mirror to study her features, she began a self-portrait but it became one of dejection and despair and so she abandoned that too. With a heavy heart she took to spending periods in her coffin, willing herself not to think about the past or the future. It was during such a withdrawal that Montigny called on her. He brought with him a play which he suggested she should consider as a vehicle for her return to the Odéon stage. When he had gone she picked up the manuscript and began reading. It was *The Lady of the Camelias.*

The younger Dumas had written *The Lady of the Camelias* a quarter of a century earlier as a novel when he was only twenty-four. Later, for want of money, he carved a play from it. Subsequently it had become a play that stock companies put on to fill up gaps between fresher offerings. Yet its very survival was testimony to the fact that it touched the soul of romantic love.

Marguerite Gautier, a spoilt Paris courtesan in the early years of the century, has never been in love. When she meets the young Armand Duval, a handsome and a refreshingly honest contrast to her usual circle, she falls deeply and sincerely in love with him. But although he is of an aristocratic family he has no money. Unbeknown to him she sells her jewels to secure them a house in the country, where for a while they live in a fool's paradise of love. He struggles somewhat ineffectually against this dependence and doting on her continues the rapturous idyll. One day, in his absence, Marguerite receives a visit from Armand's father. The old man argues that it is her duty, if she truly loves him, to give him up if only for the sake of Armand's sister who, it appears, is to marry into a family of such utter respectability that a mere mention of the liaison would wreck the prospect. Self-sacrificially – and perhaps out of a certain nostalgia for her gay former life – Marguerite agrees. She returns to Paris and her life of courtly prostitution, thus incurring Armand's hatred. He knows nothing of his father's entreaties. When they next meet it is at a party and Marguerite is surrounded by admirers. Jealously, Armand throws in her face the money he has just won at cards, but months later learns the truth. He rushes back to Paris to find her in the final stages of consumption. After tearfully restating their love for one another Marguerite has a heart attack and dies in his arms.

Unabashedly romantic, extravagantly sentimental, this piece (later to provide the plot for Verdi's *La Traviata*) is redeemable only through the artifice of the actress who plays Marguerite. Montigny knew that in the hands of a Bernhardt it would be one of the most emotionally effective pieces of theatre he had ever produced.

But when she had read it Sarah felt that to return to the theatre in such a play would amount to professional suicide. She remembered reading that a Madame Doche had first performed it at the Vaudeville in the 1850s. Subsequently it had been a staple for all manner of actresses, many of them well past their prime. Why should Montigny consider it worth reviving? It was a museum piece. The heroine's highflown principles were uncharacteristic, unbelievable. The plot relied on social conventions the war had done much to bury. A public that had experienced the realities of revolution would surely not respond favourably to a play based on an outmoded love affair. Feeling annoyed with Montigny she pushed the manuscript aside. But for some reason she could not get Marguerite out of her mind.

Her thoughts strayed back to a summer's day in the Luxembourg Gardens. 'Surely the life I can offer you is worth some sacrifice,' she heard Prince Henri saying. She thought of the bitter way in which Armand had thrown the money. 'You're nothing but a little whore!' But it was Henri who had said that!

Confused, she picked up the play again. Perhaps it needed revision, re-writing here and there. She began to see it as a skeleton upon which to build something much more true, more eloquent. For all its sentimentality it was a play about renunciation, a noble idea if the reasons were worthy. Was it ever right, she asked herself, to sacrifice fulfilment for conventions – and for someone else's conventions? Would Armand's love for Marguerite, who was older, have stood the test of time? Did Marguerite really want to change? Would she not have pined for the promiscuous life? She began to see it now as a story of an impossible love – almost in the classical tradition – a love that would have died if Marguerite had not. And what a beautiful death scene!

She began warily at first to think of what she could do with the role. To do it well she would have to tread a careful path between under- and over-playing. It was essential that the audience should be listening to what Marguerite is *thinking.* This was particularly applicable, she decided, to the letter scene.

As a scene there is hardly anything to it – it occurs after the visit of Armand's father. He has left with Marguerite's promise that she will do the noble thing and leave her lover. She sits down to write a farewell letter to Armand who is spending the day in Paris. The letter, the most difficult she has ever had to write, will be left for him to discover on his return. While writing she is interrupted by his earlier than expected return. She crumples the page, curbs her emotion, and steadies herself for the ordeal of parting. But inevitably she breaks down. After explaining away her tears she even laughs. Then, saying that she has to chat to some friends left unattended in the garden, she leaves him – for ever. It was a scene, Sarah realized, with which she could make an audience *watch* her mind at work. Not much is said, little happens. The audience has to *feel* her heartbreak at parting with such deception. The love of Armand and Marguerite had to take on an importance for the audience quite out of proportion to its merits.

The audience had to feel a sense of loss, of irreparable calamity. It would require the ultimate in technique and timing, she decided, but what a challenge! Montigny, she decided, was a wise old devil.

The following day she rose early and informed Madame Guérard that she was going to the theatre. She gave Maurice an affectionate hug and the boy went off to school with an unusually light heart. It was high time they bought new curtains for the drawing-room she suggested to Mam'selle. Why not visit the Bon Marché? Madame Guérard enthusiastically agreed; it had been a long time since Sarah had been so bright and purposeful or had taken any interest in domestic matters. Perhaps life would now return to normal.

On reaching the Odéon Sarah did not go immediately to Montigny's office. She stood in the auditorium reflectively. There were new seats of pale blue velvet, freshly moulded frescoes, a myriad of crystal chandeliers. She shut her eyes, remembering the cold, the fury of the winter, the nights when the dying screamed and shells whined overhead. To have erased so quickly all trace of it in the cause of make-believe seemed almost indecent. Then she shut out the past and went to see Montigny. 'I'll do the play,' she said. 'When do we start?'

With *The Lady of the Camelias* Sarah re-established herself in the hearts of theatre-goers: during the course of her life she would play the role over 3000 times. She had been wrong to think that the play would be spurned because it ended so sadly. Night after night the highly emotional death-scene had every woman in the house and some of the most resolute men weeping openly. It seemed to act as a release, just as effective as laughter, for the pent-up feelings of a people who had withstood the real rigours and tragedies of the siege.

Of all the death scenes she would play this would be the most theatrical, but through mastery of her art she would rend hearts with it. Even the most unromantic of spirits would feel that they had witnessed something noble. It was done by timing and technique, by the mystique which is great acting. Probably more than any other this was the performance that began to create the Bernhardt legend. For those who had seen it felt impelled to speak of it to others as if by so doing they could induce what was so ephemeral, yet so magical, to live on.

To achieve her effects, Sarah had done much more than learn the role. She had added fresh dimensions to Dumas's tinsel drama by scoring out certain lines and adding others. Her working script in which she detailed the gestures, pauses and asides looked like a draughtsman's notes for an intricate technological construction. To give the dying Marguerite an essential authenticity she had consulted the medical profession about the effects of consumption. She had learned that in its final feverish stages it tends to heighten feelings of sexual passion. She verified that it would take about thirty seconds from the moment Marguerite's heart stopped for her spinal cord to cease to support her. She could thus allow precisely that time for her whole body to slump and her arm to slip from Armand's shoulder, after, of course, her final speech: 'Give me your hand. It's not difficult to die, I assure you. I'm not suffering any more. Life is pouring into me. I'm going to live! Armand, I love you!'

Doctors who saw the performance said that they became quite uncomfortable. Before her expiry she had made that room seem positively germ-laden. But they were impressed by the veracity of it all. There was, in fact, no resisting such acting. It had the power and sincerity of life – and death – about it.

Sarah emerged from *The Lady of the Camelias* a prodigious and shining star. At thirty she was the leading actress of the Paris theatre and she began to live the part in real life too. She had a house built for her on the

Boulevard de Clichy. Here she installed all the belongings from her apartment and added more. They were of a similarly flamboyant kind so that in the end her home had the same ambience – sensuous, colourful, over-furnished – only more so. Georges Clarin, who had painted a portrait of her posing on her famous divan, decorated the ceiling of her bedroom. She prevailed upon other artist friends to paint murals in the foyer and dining-room. One room was again set aside as a studio for her sculpting and painting for in both these arts she had gained recognition. She had been offered several lucrative commissions, including one to sculpt the head of a Rothschild, but it was through her celebrity as an actress that she was able to exploit these creative talents.

Once settled in the new house she engaged a domestic staff including a coachman, who was always liveried, and Emile, an eighteen-year-old houseboy. She began to entertain lavishly. There were luncheon parties, five o'clock 'at homes' and dinner parties if she were free. Those who came to her house were, in the main, writers and politicians, not actors, for by now she was indisputably the most celebrated figure in the French theatre and she thought that other actors would come simply to bathe in the renown she had worked so hard to achieve. An exception was the beautiful but not over-talented Marie Colombier. More than once Marie had spoken of giving up the theatre in favour of writing, an aspiration Sarah humoured but considered unrealistic. She didn't believe Marie had the intelligence. She still was impressed by Marie's ability to attract men yet be quite incapable of sustaining a relationship with any other than the least imaginative of them. For all the extrovert requirements of her vocation, Sarah was a shy person with whom it was not always easy to communicate. In addition, her fame caused a certain isolation from the less illustrious. Through Marie she was able to meet more ordinary mortals who made it less lonely at the top.

In her public life, according to Maurice Rostand, son of the poet and playwright, she could be 'unjust, angry, capricious, unbearable, contradictory, provocative, rebellious, intransigent, but never petty'. But in her private life she had a need for intimacy that often went unmet because strangers were nervous of the image created by her public reputation. It was a dilemma that was to handicap her search for personal happiness and make the adoration of the public all the more important.

During the run of *The Lady of the Camelias* Sarah began to feel the need of a partner. Despite success, admiration, a host of stimulating friends, there were times when she felt disturbingly alone. The role of Marguerite left her with a longing. Marriage was a concept she had deliberately thrust aside when deciding to succeed in her career. Now Henri's proposal kept coming back. At the end of a night's performance she felt drained. All she desired was to return home and sleep. Then, once in bed, her mind became active and sleep eluded her.

Madame Guérard understood. One night when the two women sat up talking she told Sarah that she should get married, that her life had become unnatural. 'You have power over others,' said Mam'selle, 'you can enchant them with a glance, but nobody must have power over you. That is the reason for your loneliness.' Sarah was at once on the defensive. Only Mam'selle would presume to talk to her in this way and Sarah knew she meant well. But it was one's duty to be whole; happiness did not come from dependence. Yet she did feel an unease; there was no one with whom to share the main burdens of success.

Success *was* proving a burden. As France's premier actress everything she did made news. She was never able to screen her private life from the curiosity of the Press. Publicity, in fact, spoiled her affair with Georges Clarin. She began to suspect him of using it to gain publicity for himself. Who else could have told the Press that his painting on her bedroom ceiling depicted her own nude body gambolling among fleecy clouds? She and Georges had been very close. They had a similarly volatile disposition, loving acclaim, spurning the conventional. But the gossipy weeklies seized on the affair and made it public property. They were accused of giving dubious parties at his studio for art students and actresses. At one a newspaper claimed she had appeared in the nude, her body painted suggestively by Clarin. Publicity of this kind drew letters of abuse from the public. No matter how vociferously she denied these assertions, or resorted to legal action, there grew up alongside her reputation as an actress of genius the image of a woman of no moral principles.

'They delight in sticking knives into me,' she declared publicly on one occasion. 'I hate them. They tear down gods, these little people of the yellow Press. Riff-raff! Let them talk. They think they are throwing stones at me, but every stone goes to help in building the structure of my success.' This was undeniable – the more they ranted against her the more famous she became. But even Sarah, who valued publicity, was dumbfounded at times by the venom of some of the attacks. When Angelo, the good-looking Italian boy who played Armand, became her lover the Press soon knew about it. Sarah had warned her domestic staff that if they gossiped to journalists they would be instantly dismissed.

Angelo was only eighteen. She had chosen him for the role because an age difference between Armand and Marguerite seemed intrinsic. Angelo was excellent in the role and she decided to help his career by introducing him to some of her friends. After one of her dinner parties he remained when the others had left. It was clear that he was offering to share her bed. With the zeal of his race he proved to be the kind of lover who satisfied her need to be possessed completely. It was an affair without commitment, each appreciative of the pleasure they found in one another, and Angelo was not infrequently seen entering her house.

The Press devoured the liaison. Sarah was pictured as a woman of nymphomanic tastes. Such stories packed the theatre but were painful to her privately. Women whose lives were more restricted than Sarah's sometimes wrote letters intended to wound – and they were successful. Another unhappy outcome of journalistic malice was that Maurice was taunted at school. He got into occasional affrays in her defence. In vain Sarah fought back at the Press: 'They say I am selfish – well, what woman is not? They say I am greedy – but did you ever know me to have a spare franc I could call my own? They say I am cold and haughty, but that is because I will not suffer the presence of fools! They say I am indiscreet – it is they who are indiscreet! They say I have never really loved, that I am cruel and ambitious, that I pull men down and climb over their bodies on my ascent to fame – *it is not true!* I am ambitious, yes, and I am jealous of a success won by hard work; but I am haughty only to those whom I despise, and I am cruel – never. It is they who are cruel to me!' But the glare of such publicity was inhibiting and she saw less and less of Angelo outside theatre hours. Soon she was alone again.

At a time when the struggle for female emancipation had only just begun she was living in open defiance of the conventions. A host of women saw this as a brave symbol but just as many strongly disapproved. So controversial a public figure was a gift to publicists. Her extreme slenderness and that riot of red hair made her easy to caricature. Imperiously she argued back when journalists questioned her right to live her own life. At dinner parties she was listened to with respect. But the strain of being a hostess was considerable – especially without a host. At the end of an evening who was there to talk to? Neither Mam'selle nor Maurice could contribute much sophistication. After hours at the theatre coming home to a housekeeper and a small boy was scarcely satisfying. Could a marriage solve the problem of that special kind of loneliness which inflicts the committed, the uncompromising? Or would it simply be a way of silencing her critics?

The question was hypothetical; there was no one in her life. Nevertheless, Mam'selle had accurately discerned that her craving to be with people, her succession of affairs were impermanent subterfuges. Far too often now she felt vulnerable and alone.

CHAPTER 13

After the hundredth performance of *The Lady of the Camelias* Montigny gave a spectacular party. He wanted it nostalgically to evoke memories of the glittering balls of what now seemed the far off days of the Second Empire.

Life under the Third Republic had been consciously austere, a reaction to the ostentations of the Napoleonic court, but Montigny believed the public still liked to read about glamorous people. He wanted the reception to recall the froth and brilliance of the old society and he took over the Café Hardy for the occasion.

Leading figures in the administration were invited, as were members of the diplomatic corps. Celebrities in the arts, the theatre critics and the more reputable journalists were also asked for he wanted to reap a benefit in prestige for the Odéon. Attendance by his actors and actresses was obligatory and each was permitted to bring a guest.

Inevitably Sarah's entrance, which was well after that of everyone else, was the climax. Montigny had every reason to be proud of his star. Having just bewitched her audience she had changed at the theatre into an elegant black evening gown designed by Worth. She carried red roses and as she moved across the salon she presented these one by one to guests who received them with gestures of homage as if she were a queen. Before she took her seat at the long table where Montigny, Sardou and other guests were, everyone in the salon rose. The ovation lasted until it was seen that she had sat down – and then the orchestra began a waltz.

Amid this adulation Sarah noticed someone at her table who appeared pointedly detached from it. His bored expression was so much in contrast to the general mood of those around him that it presented a challenge. He would have interested her anyway because he was exceptionally handsome. 'Who is the man with Marie?' she asked Sardou.

'Do Marie's lovers need names?' he replied, an answer which irritated her. The more she looked at him the more interested she became. Black hair, insolent features. His mouth was sensuous but rather weak.

'He is an attaché at the Greek Embassy,' said Montigny.

Sarah decided to be imperious. 'Since when am I not introduced to guests at my table?'

'It's hardly worth introducing you, my dear Sarah,' said Sardou. 'He was kicked out of Greece. He's about to be kicked out of France.' He raised his glass in a toast to her, encouraging the others to do likewise. 'To our divine Sarah.'

She acknowledged it absently. The one person at the table who had not raised his glass was the man beside Marie. He had continued to smoke a cigar.

'What were his crimes? Why does this Greek attaché have to leave so many countries?'

Still Sardou wanted to distract her. 'He's a notorious lady-killer. One look is enough, surely. A weak-willed Don Juan, a gigolo.' But every word he spoke intensified her interest. Suddenly she stood up and leant across the table. 'Marie . . . introduce me to your young friend.'

Marie looked up in surprise. 'Of course,' she said uncertainly but made the introduction. 'Madame Bernhardt – Monsieur Aristide Damala.'

Damala rose formally and bowed.

'Thank you, Monsieur,' she said. 'I would love to dance.' He had not invited her. Dismayed, Marie sensed the awkwardness of the situation. She watched Damala move to the floor. Deliberately, he kept her waiting while he extinguished his cigar. Then, rather ungraciously, he took

Sarah into the dance.

'You have taken a vow of silence,' she said after some time.

Damala thought this over. 'It is a great responsibility to dance with Madame Bernhardt.'

She ignored the sarcasm. 'I dance well?'

'Madame does everything well, I'm sure.'

'Then perhaps you would have asked me to dance – later.'

'Surely, you have enough handsome admirers.'

'So you are handsome, Monsieur?'

He faltered slightly. 'I have been told so.'

'But you don't believe everything you are told.'

They danced in silence. Then he said: 'Why are you trying to score off me, Madame?'

'Because you interest me. Because I have had a wonderful success and you are the only one I have failed to impress. Just look at my friends at the table over there – beautiful, talented, loyal, loving. I know them backwards. But you are uncharted, a sea I would like to sail in for a while.'

'Am I supposed to feel flattered?'

'You don't understand,' she said a little bitterly. 'An attaché? Frock coat, spats, a little case and a big head.'

The waltz was over. She expected him to leave. Instead he spoke calmly. 'What I wear in my work is as much a costume as the one you wear on a stage. We are all actors on occasion.'

'You act?'

'I have thought about it.'

'Is that why you were determined to attract my attention by ignoring me?'

For the first time he smiled. 'Have I succeeded?'

'Come and see me tomorrow afternoon.' She gave him her address. 'I will tell you all about acting.'

Damala escorted her back to the head of the table, then returned to his place beside Marie. Both Sardou and

Montigny watched her intently. She felt trapped by these well-meaning friends. Her eyes were on Damala and she noted how relaxed he was with Marie. Sardou wanted to tell her more about the young Greek. He had been involved in scandal at St Petersburg – the wife of a Czarist government minister had committed suicide. In Athens a girl of eighteen had tried to shoot him. In Paris the staff of his mission called him 'the diplomatic Apollo'. But a reputation as a philanderer was one thing; more serious rumour claimed that he was sadistic. It had been suggested that he took morphine. But if these assertions had been made she would not have believed them. She deplored gossip. No one knew more how cruel it could be. Damala was probably insecure and bored with his job. The nonchalant, surly, slightly mocking manner he had adopted was a façade. While they danced she sensed how tense he was. He had a vibrancy but it was constricted. She understood that. Perhaps she could lead him to a creative release. Without doubt he was one of the most physically desirable men she had ever set eyes on. Now he was being monopolized by Marie and she found that unbearable. 'I am going home,' she told Sardou.

For the first time in her life she was jealous. Because the feeling was new she neither recognized it nor had any defence against it. Up to now the men she had wanted had also found her desirable. They had even been flattered. What was different about Damala was his apparent lack of interest in her. Yet she refused to believe that this could be due to a preference for Marie. Perhaps her influential position meant nothing to him as it would have done had he been an actor.

As she tried to sleep that night these thoughts disturbed her. And it wasn't just of Damala she was thinking. What haunted her was the thought that Marie was with him, that he might be making love to her. In vain she told herself that in a few hours she would see him when he called as arranged. For each moment held the spectre of the two of them together, his powerful, well-proportioned body, her voluptuous, willing one. She realized that she wanted Damala more than she had wanted anyone in her whole life. Only the coming of daylight calmed her so she was able to fall asleep.

At mid-morning she awoke alert to the prospect of the day. She would be seeing Damala. She had time for no one else. She told Emile to take Maurice for a pony ride. She was edgy with Mam'selle. By afternoon she had dressed in the silk trouser-suit in which she felt most relaxed. Her nerves were taut. She moved from room to room changing the position of chairs, vases, photographs, sometimes restoring them to where they had originally been. She wanted to create the impression of someone not just intellectual but also simple, informal, easy to please. Although she hated visitors to smoke she placed beside a favourite armchair a box of the very finest cigars.

When the doorbell sounded she instantly sat down, picked up a book and pretended to read. It was not Damala. A maid brought her a note. It was from Victor Hugo. Oh, damn the old buffoon. She steadied herself. Hugo, it seemed, had been in the audience the night before. The message was one of homage. France's Grand Old Man of Letters wrote: 'You moved me. I wept. This tear is yours,' and in a little box accompanying the note was a diamond pendant in the shape of a tear.

Sarah was in no mood to appreciate the great man's gesture. The doorbell rang a second time. Damala? The maid announced Alphonse de Rothschild. Sarah said she would see him in the studio. He had come to inspect the head of him she was sculpting. He bowed and kissed her hand. Then he saw the unfinished bust. 'My God! Is that supposed to be me?' he said. Sarah's nerves snapped. She picked up the statue and hurled it to the floor. 'It *was* supposed to be,' she said. 'Now it's a heap of rubble.' She felt guilty. 'My friend, you came at a bad time. I am bored. *Bored!* I have a wild desire to do something utterly different, to travel perhaps. I want to see different landscapes, other skies. Oh, I want to breathe a different air! Help me!'

'Calm yourself, Sarah,' said the great financier. 'You have my sympathy.' His eyes twinkled. A visit to the irascible Sarah took his mind off more sombre concerns, like the raising of all that money France was paying Germany. 'You know, in Paris we are all suffering from claustrophobia. Why not take a trip in a balloon! Is that different enough?'

She burst out laughing. 'You know, it is a really excellent idea.'

When Rothschild left she got ready for the theatre. Her disappointment was combined with regret. She had cheapened herself by inviting Damala in the way that she had done. It had probably made him the more loyal to Marie. At the theatre she was sullen and gave a bad performance. Afterwards at supper with Sardou she mentioned Rothschild's suggestion of a balloon trip. Sardou thought the notion delightful and promised to arrange a flight.

A few days later they rode to a clearing in the Bois de Boulogne. An impressive orange hot-air balloon had been prepared for ascent. When she stepped into the gondola she saw with pleasure that he had stocked it with a food hamper and bottles of champagne. Her companions on the trip were to be Sardou and a Monsieur Tissandier, an experienced balloonist. Inevitably, the newspapers had heard of her plan but she refused interviews. She asked Monsieur Tissandier to start the ascent. As they left the ground she saw a carriage enter the clearing at speed. From it jumped Montigny. He waved to her angrily. 'Come back,' he shouted. 'This is an irresponsible risk.' But by then they were ascending rapidly.

The first thing that impressed her was the total silence. Out of earshot of voices from the ground there was nothing to distract her. The sight of Paris revealing herself was inspiring. Up and up they soared with the city glistening under a faint blue mist. To see it from such an angle was a marvel. Freed from its clamour she could view objectively this stage on which her life had been performed. Sardou pointed out the Odéon. It was only then that she remembered that it was a day of two performances. There was a special matinée. But there was nothing she could do about it now. This brief freedom was essential. Montigny hadn't realized the strain she had lived under, the disciplines of a long run, the constant scrutiny of the public and the Press. Nor had he ever made allowance for the fact that she had no partner to shield her from such pressures. She was thinking of Damala when the balloon suddenly plunged into clouds and she felt their soothing milky vapour on her skin.

At a thousand feet they were moving across a fairyland fringed with orange from the evening sun, and in this setting they decided to have their supper. Sardou opened the champagne, popping the corks into the abundant air, and they ate pâté de foie gras, crusty bread and delicious black grapes. It was a long time since she had felt so alive. But above a thousand feet it began to be cold; night was falling. She felt uncomfortable and very drowsy. A strong wind rose and blew them further eastwards. By now it was freezing. Her ears blocked, her nose began to bleed, and Tissandier, seeing her distress, opened the valves to start the descent. At first he aimed at a clearing in a wood but the wind made piloting difficult. The clouds, now above them, had turned an ugly grey; in the gathering darkness a storm was brewing. At a hundred feet they threw out the grapple ropes but the balloon missed the clearing and came to rest on the platform of a country station.

Sarah climbed out of the gondola. Once on firm ground again she was less shaky than either Sardou or Tissandier.

They were some forty-odd miles east of Paris. They had to find the station master and enquire about trains. He was in his office having supper. Understandably, he was amazed to see these well-dressed Parisians appear so unexpectedly. He told them there was no train from his small station that night. If they were to go to Ermenonville, some eight or so miles further east away from Paris, there on the main rail line there would be a train at midnight. It would mean a good two-hour walk. He doubted whether city people could walk that far and offered them some bread and cheese. Sarah was determined to try and so France's most illustrious actress, her most successful playwright and their aeronaut (abashed by his unmeritorious descent) began the long walk to Ermenonville. They arrived mudded and soaked to the skin but caught the train to Paris. Half dead with fatigue Sarah reached home at 4 a.m. to find Madame Guérard in a state of anxiety. Montigny's secretary had called at the house several times. Finally he had left a note. In it Sarah read that Montigny wanted to see her in his office at the Odéon that morning.

Stories of the flight appeared in the morning newspapers. One noted her failure to appear at two performances at the Odéon. Another carried a drawing by an illustrator. From a gondola high above Paris Sarah was shown pointing down at the Odéon; her other arm was around Sardou. The caption read: 'Sarah looks down on Paris – should Paris look up to her?'

The editorials in several newspapers were critical of her life-style. The balloon exploit, said one, was 'another example of this incredible lady's intention to shock us'. She was not merely eccentric, she was outrageous. Another pontificated about whether or not a woman 'who flies in the face of convention' (were they conscious of the pun?) was 'a tolerable example to the womanhood of a city trying so hard to reconstruct itself soberly, laboriously and unselfishly'. All these stories, Sarah noted, were written by men.

But the most wounding of them all was by a woman who had signed herself 'A Humble Actress'. This dishonest article took the opportunity of the balloon adventure to resurrect calumnies from the past and invent several more. It painted a picture of a woman of alarming extravagance and eccentricity. She bathed in milk and had ordered a coach and four in gold and ebony. She had slapped Montigny's face. She had been seen on the boulevards with the young Prince Louis Bonaparte (who, in fact, was in England and would shortly die in Zululand). She was working secretly for the restoration of the monarchy. She had an unquenchable appetite for strong drink. Her neighbours had been forced to move due to the noxious smell from her menagerie. She was not a woman at all but a man masquerading in woman's clothes who frequented disreputable dance halls and picked up girls for pleasure. Sarah was appalled. Could such lies have been invented by anyone she knew? Madame Nathalie? Angry, hurt, dispirited and having had no sleep she left for her meeting with Montigny.

Montigny came quickly to the point. 'Your contract distinctly states that without permission you are not supposed to go out of Paris.'

'Up is not out,' said Sarah. 'I went above Paris. How could I know how far the wind would carry me?'

'If you hadn't been *up* there it couldn't have carried you anywhere. You missed two performances.'

'Blame it on the breeze. I needed to get away.'

'You are up to your old tricks again. I made you a star and you think you can get away with anything. You have a duty to the theatre. Besides, you have made me look ridiculous.' (A cartoon in one of the newspapers had depicted Montigny dressed as a Prussian sniper trying to shoot the balloon down.) He continued more calmly: 'You owe me your success, Sarah. You had an obligation to me. Do you want to ruin the Odéon with your insanities?'

It was more than she could accept. 'I owe my success to no one,' she said. 'I am under no obligation to anyone. I have brought prestige to your theatre. Now it has become a prison for me. I might as well be tied to your proscenium, always there, always well enough to perform. Well, I can't be taken entirely for granted. I've had enough. I can't have every moment of my life restricted. I have to breathe, to be free.' Before Montigny could stop her she was leaving. 'I resign,' she shouted and slammed the door behind her.

Within minutes both regretted what had happened, but neither would have the humility to say so. They would never work together again.

Sarah, who was always a misery to live with when not working, during the weeks that followed taxed Madame Guérard's patience to the hilt. For the first time in twenty years this gentle creature thought of leaving. But for Maurice she probably would have done. The restless actress developed such a hostility to life that it bore down the household. Mam'selle wondered if Sarah was on the brink of a breakdown. The studio daily became more littered with plaster, brushes, mallets, chisels, canvasses, but despite much frantic activity nothing got done. A work that appeared to be proceeding promisingly would suddenly be smashed on the floor. No callers were admitted. Food was left on trays and she took to going out at night alone. Sometimes she returned with new acquaintances and entertained them until dawn.

One morning Madame Guérard found her in the studio with an old woman. 'Look at her eyes,' said Sarah. 'Look at the sadness there. That is what I want to capture. I'm going to do a head of her.' To Madame Guérard the woman looked like many to be found in the slum quarters, except that this one might be mad. Her eyes had a crazed and crafty look. Sarah insisted on telling Mam'selle her story.

The woman was a Bretonese and had lost five sons, all sailors. Two had been killed by the Germans in 1870, three had been drowned. She had adopted the little son of her youngest boy, always keeping him away from the sea, teaching him to fear the water. But the youngster developed a disease of the bones for which a doctor prescribed sea water. Reluctantly, the grandmother took the boy to the coast and sat on the sands while he paddled. But she fell asleep. On waking she saw him drifting out to sea in a small boat. Frantically she called to him, but a mist rose and soon the boat was out of sight. She never saw the boy again.

'As you can see,' said Sarah, 'she is quite mad.'

Madame Guérard had never heard anything so maudlin. She was relieved when Sarah lost interest in the project, paid the woman money and sent her away. But the incident was symptomatic of Sarah's deepening depression.

Each day brought new concerns. One evening after dinner Sarah told Mam'selle that she intended to go to bed, but the following morning her bedroom was discovered to be empty. Alarmed, Mam'selle waited, praying that she had come to no harm. When Sarah returned she was wearing male attire – a striped suit, white shirt and grey cravat – and presumably had been out all night. Madame Guérard decided to talk seriously to her. That afternoon at five she took tea into the studio and waited.

'What is it?' Sarah asked.

'I must speak to you, Sarah,' said Mam'selle. 'You are behaving so strangely. Even Maurice is troubled. He knows something is wrong. And you are not looking well.'

Sarah sat down beside her. 'You have known me a long time, ma petite dame,' she said, 'but does anyone really know me?'

'What do you mean?'

'You read the newspapers.'

'You mean you are making their terrible lies come true? It is yourself you are hurting – and those who love you.'

'Have you read what they write? Really read them?' She was bitterly upset. 'I am a Bonapartist, a traitor, a woman of strange tastes, a transvestite, no morals. I am cruel. I starve my animals and corrupt the young. I do all that. Yet I stayed in Paris when others fled. I nursed the sick. I cleansed their wounds and fed them. I lifted their wretched spirits at the cost of my own. I've given away more than I've ever spent on myself. Where is the sense in it? What's the use of working? I'm no longer interested in their opinions. I'll live the way they think I live.' She was in tears.

Madame Guérard took her hand. 'There is more to your unhappiness than that, Sarah,' she said. 'You have been libelled by the Press many times before and it hasn't caused you this kind of suffering. You are making yourself miserable for quite another reason.'

'I don't know what you're talking about.'

'I'm talking about Monsieur Damala. The young man who intended to call.'

She shrugged.

'Just because one man refuses to pay attention to you . . .'

'I don't want to talk about it.'

'Then come to your senses. Remember who you are. One of the most gifted people alive.'

'I'm also a human being.'

'But don't bury yourself in self-pity. What can a man with a cheap talent for seduction ever really mean to you? You are unique. I've said enough.' She rose, but Sarah pulled her back. Now they were both in tears.

That evening Sarah had a caller whom Madame Guérard persuaded her to see. Edward Jarrett had travelled from London. He was England's most successful impresario. He had heard that Sarah's association with the Odéon had ended. Would she appear in London? She could select her company, choose her own repertory and within reason name her own price. He knew about her preference for payment in gold. Would 200 gold sovereigns for each performance be adequate? A London house, of course, would be provided. Quite by chance he happened to have on him a contract which set out these terms. He had even brought a gold fountain-pen, a token of the British public's esteem.

'By the way,' Jarrett asked as she put her signature to the contract. 'Have you any names in mind as supporting players?'

'Well,' said Sarah thoughtfully, 'there's only one that immediately springs to mind.'

'I'll see that he or she's engaged.'

'Her name,' said Sarah, 'is Marie Colombier.'

CHAPTER 14

In the 1870s Europeans regarded England in the same way as they would regard America in the 1920s and 1930s – as by far the richest country in the world. The biggest and the latest were to be found there. London was the largest city in the western world. Visitors from the Continent to the British capital commented on the hurry and thrust of its citizens, their relentless pursuit of commerce and talk of money. In much the same way Europeans would speak of the feel of New York half a century later.

A French visitor in the 1870s thought that a notice he had seen in many London offices – 'You are requested to speak of business matters only' – dauntingly emphasized the fact that work had become a cult in Victorian England. For the owners and managers of industry, the exporters, shippers and middlemen, as well as for a rapidly emergent middle class, the industrial revolution had paid off handsomely. But for those who had been exploited in the process it had created, side by side with the wealth and magnificence, social conditions where, as Henry James observed, 'Immensity was the great fact . . . the low black houses were as inanimate as so many rows of coal scuttles, save where at frequent corners, from a gin shop, there was a flare of light more brutal still than the darkness.'

It was this baleful glimpse of London that Sarah first obtained as the boat train from Folkestone made its way through miles and miles of house-tops, viaducts and complications of junctions and signals in its approach to Charing Cross. The weather had turned wet. Coal smuts in the drizzle coated the carriage windows with a grime like sooty snow.

The journey from Paris had been full of incident. Rising early she had said a tearful farewell to Maurice and Madame Guérard while thirteen carriage trunks and hatboxes were stowed into two landaus. Despite the hour a group of well-wishers had assembled at the Gare du Nord to see her off. At Calais there was another crowd which included a young man of wild appearance who presented her with his newest invention. It was an inflatable lifebelt in which there were water-tight compartments containing phials of brandy. Should Sarah be shipwrecked, he said, she could leap into the sea wearing the lifebelt. But she should be sure to carry a pin with which to pierce the pockets containing the brandy. Thus equipped she could stay alive for hours. When relieved of this madman Sarah transferred to the Channel boat for her first sea voyage.

After her tour had been reported in the Paris Press she had received from members of the public all manner of medicaments against *mal de mer*. The French hypochondriac attitude to the sea-crossing was well known. But her devoted fans need not have worried for the crossing was a calm one and she stepped on to the quayside at Folkestone radiant.

Sarah's much publicized career had been followed with close interest by sophisticated elements in London. In some circles an expression was current to describe attitudes or behaviour designed to shock – 'Who do you think you are? Sarah Bernhardt?' – and in time this saying would permeate by way of the music-halls right down the social scale into the fruitier vernacular of the cockney. But her reputation had not only preceded her, it had been given an additional shine by the advance drum-beating of the publicity-conscious Jarrett. As a result she arrived at Folkestone to find a crowd of welcomers that included Oscar Wilde, himself never averse to news-making. He held an armful of white lilies which he scattered on the ground for her to walk upon. This was the first step in a friendship that was to continue beyond Wilde's rejection and imprisonment to his exile and death in France. It would be marred somewhat by Sarah's neglect of him at the hour of his need but Wilde would dedicate his play *Salome* to her. After stepping on Wilde's lilies she accepted a far less flamboyant offering in the form of a tiny bunch of violets from a handsome young actor named Johnston Forbes-Robertson. In later years he would be a performer of great calibre and one of the finest Hamlets of all time. Encouraged by this star treatment and with shouts of 'Vive Bernhardt!' in the early twilight she boarded the train for London. Once settled in her compartment she brooded over something removed from this adulation and brouhaha, but it was as intriguing. At the interchange at Folkestone she had discovered that travelling on the train with Marie Colombier was Aristide Damala.

As the train puttered its way across the fields of Kent, Sarah turned over in her mind the implications of this circumstance. It had not come as a complete surprise to her. Damala, she knew, had been living with Marie. It was what had prompted Sarah to invite her to join the tour. She could have left him in Paris or asked permission to bring him along. Marie had made no such request and by bringing him without authorization she was in conflict with the rules of the tour which made no provision for travelling companions. Once in London she would have to deal with the matter.

If anyone in the company required the support of a companion, she reasoned, it was herself. She had the main responsibility for the success of the London season. It was not to be treated by a subordinate member of her company as an amorous excursion! Such musings occupied her as they travelled deeper into England.

Night had brought a bleak mixture of dampness and chill. Soon the enviable glow of homesteads in the neat fields, where sheep grazed in deepening shadows, gave way to suburbia and the new estates of Eltham, Peckham and Camberwell where the respectable middle classes had settled into solid terrace homes close to the railway, Europe's first commuters. Then they were crossing Hungerford Bridge through whose network of iron she could see London's river with its masted traffic crowding into the busiest port on earth, its bridges burgeoning with horse traffic and people.

Towering above all, dwarfing the myriad of Wren steeples and smoke-stacks and spires, was the durable silhouette of St Paul's.

London, she decided, had none of the symmetrical elegance of Haussmann's Paris but what a mighty power was there. Through industrial supremacy, ruthless diplomacy and force of arms this city claimed dominion over half the world.

As the train slipped between the platforms at Charing Cross the awesome nature of her responsibility as an artiste come to entertain pushed aside more personal thoughts such as how she would react on encountering Damala. She was thrilled to see that the station authorities had laid out a red carpet for her.

No sooner had the train come to a halt than Jarrett, looking very businesslike in a bowler, entered the compartment. He came to brief her on the arrangements for her arrival – 'A small welcoming speech from a representative of the management of the Gaiety Theatre, a Press conference at the house in Chester Square (which Lord Northrop had put at her disposal) and later a reception by the Duke and Duchess of Kent . . .' Sarah liked Jarrett's brisk efficiency but wasn't something wrong? Despite the red carpet there was no crowd. She asked him why and he had to tell her. The red carpet was for the Prince of Wales who had left that afternoon on the boat train to Paris. She put further questions to the representative from the Gaiety, cutting his speech of welcome short in midstream. The Prince would not be in residence, she learnt, for part of the London season but he had delegated to his brother, the Duke of Connaught, the use of the Royal Box. Doubtless the Duke would put in an appearance at some time. Sarah's mood darkened. The warmth of her welcome at Folkestone had led her to expect far more. She began walking to the head of the train in a black humour. A distinctly unnerved Jarrett remained at her side. In this frame of mind her progress was blocked by Damala helping Marie from the train. 'I seem to know your face, Monsieur,' she said stonily.

'Aristide Damala, Madame.' He was perfectly self-assured.

'You were coming to see me one afternoon.' Marie waited helpless, ignored. 'I expected you to arrive, Monsieur Damala.'

'I found I had a previous engagement.'

'Yet you sent no note of apology.'

Although her voice had the bite of a whiplash Damala refused to cringe. 'I felt that your invitation was given on the spur of the moment and that you would have forgotten it by morning.'

'What are you doing in England? Has your Embassy transferred you here?'

'No, Madame.'

'Dismissed you?'

'I have left the foreign service,' he said.

'And where are you staying in London?'

'He is staying with me, Madame,' said Marie, feeling no triumph as she said it. No one could have felt more insecure. Damala stepped aside, Marie moved off the red carpet and Sarah continued her progress to the main hall. She halted once for a photographer, *persuaded* there she had no doubt by the cajolings of the Gaiety, and after a dazzling professional smile proceeded in a mood of black anger into the city beyond.

'When I arrive at wherever you have seen fit to put me,'

she told Jarrett icily, 'I want to see that man at once. I make the rules for my company.'

Jarrett said nothing. A long career in international management had taught him how to live with temperament. He had brought singers and ballerinas and actresses of awesome talent and celebrity across too many frontiers not to know that inside every performer of stature was a frail human being liable to break out. Invariably the reason was a variation on a simple theme: greatness came in one kind of wrapping and its colour was loneliness.

As the brougham moved from the station forecourt into Trafalgar Square on its way to Belgravia, Sarah looked sullenly out of the window, resenting the proud city, regretting that she had come. All the public monuments seemed to honour men who had vanquished the French. Nevertheless, the look of the crowds made her envious. They had the bearing of a free people whatever their condition or class. The fine vistas of well-cared-for buildings down Whitehall (with the monument to Wellington at the end) and the Strand reminded her of the look of Paris before the shelling. There was a fine elegance too about the Quadrant at Regent Street where Nash had achieved a symmetry to equal the best of Haussmann and her spirit rose higher as they entered the tree-lined dignity of Chester Square.

The brougham drew up at number 77, a house of sturdy charm, and on entering the brilliantly lit hall she saw banks of flowers with welcoming messages. Pinned to one bouquet was a card on which was written: 'Welcome – Henry Irving.'

Her mood further brightened as one of the servants led her to the drawing-room which she found to be tastefully furnished and had a huge coal-fire in an immense grate enclosed by a brass fender. She was shown the garden. Damp and misty but a garden nonetheless. This was followed by a tour of the upper rooms which pleased her and put her in a much better frame of mind.

Still determined but less belligerent she told Jarrett to send Damala to her.

'You'll see him soon,' said Jarrett, misjudging the degree of her resolve.

'I want to see him now,' she said.

He tried again: 'But there is so much to do.'

'Send Damala to me immediately.' He was never to misread her mind again.

She then agreed to see the Press. Thirty-seven journalists crowded into the drawing-room. It became acrid with tobacco smoke and the smell of damp clothing. But Sarah patiently and professionally dealt with their questions. Most wanted to know what she thought of London but as she had so far seen so little she parried the question to Jarrett who said she was greatly impressed by it.

The English Press treated her respectfully. They had long admired her wayward reputation. But one question caused apprehension, especially as it came from the London correspondent of *Le Figaro*. 'Which of the many sides of Sarah will London be treated to?' the correspondent asked in English. Jarrett translated and thinking it had been distorted in the process she replied with a list of the roles she would be performing. But the journalist repeated the question in French this time and its barbed nature became clear.

With an intimidating smile she replied to the question. 'I think I know what you mean, Monsieur, and although there are many sides to Bernhardt your newspaper has invented several more. If the public likes to believe bad things about me I suppose it is because they are often more amusing than the good ones. But I sincerely hope that the English public will not believe what the French papers say, for if they do they will be very disappointed. I have come here to entertain. My own country's journalists have found my private life more interesting. I regret that. I do not hate them for it; hatred is too fatiguing. I try to be indifferent. I forgive, but I do not forget. Gentlemen, good night.' She bowed slightly and left the room.

In her bedroom she told the maid that she would rest for an hour. If a visitor called he was to wait in the drawing-room.

When she entered the room he did not immediately see her. He was seated facing the window looking out on to the square with its black central statue and horizon dominated by an ugly church. A haze blurred the street lamps, a carriage waited in the rain. With one hand he tapped quietly on a table, the other held an unlit cigarette. For a few moments she stood and looked at him, noting the shapely curve of his shoulders, the slenderness of his waist, the way a soft gloss of hair tapered to his neck, and the light olive texture of his skin. No other man had ever looked so attractive. She let herself imagine that he belonged nowhere else but in that room with her.

Sensing her presence he turned. Frowning slightly, he stood up and bowed. She liked the way he moved, the finely contoured limbs and the virile confidence of his features. No wonder other men maligned him; they could be as jealous as women. She found herself beginning apologetically. 'I am so sorry, Monsieur, to bring you here tonight, but I felt I had to say something very urgently to you . . .'

It didn't sound convincing; she tried to be more composed. 'You see, I make the rules for my company and I cannot allow hangers-on to disturb the routine of this visit.' It was insulting and she tried to be more pleasant. 'Do you wish to smoke?'

He smiled amiably. 'Perhaps you would prefer me not to.'

His good manners disconcerted her. She thought she should explain why she disliked tobacco smoke, its effect upon her voice, but she simply said, 'Thank you.'

Then he took the initiative. 'You know,' he said, 'you could have written me a note to explain your policy. Surely a note would have served.'

Was he insinuating that she had made it an excuse to see him? She struggled to regain command. 'Certainly I could have written, but I prefer to say what I have said to your face. We are a hard-working company. We do not spend our days . . .'

She checked herself in time but it was no use.

'Love-making?' he suggested.

He was making a fool of her. 'If you put it that way. I want you to know that no one will be allowed to upset the discipline of my artistes – and your reputation, Monsieur, suggests that you are capable to doing exactly that.'

'My papers are in order, Madame. I have a right to travel where I please. I have not been kicked out of France as you suggested at the station. I have left the diplomatic service. It was never what I wanted to do. But if I had gone back to Greece I would have missed the opportunity of a lifetime.'

Had Marie become important to him? The idea was not believable.

'If I had gone back to Greece,' he continued, 'you would not have been able to teach me how to act. I think you made me that promise?'

This was cajolery, she decided.

'Are you not learning from Marie?'

He looked at her with languid self-assurance. 'There are hundreds of Maries, Madame, but there is only one Sarah Bernhardt.'

'So you count your conquests in hundreds. What do you suggest?'

'That you invite me to join your troupe.'

'We are not a circus.'

'The Sarah Bernhardt Company. Let me join and I will

no longer be, as you put it, a hanger-on.'

'I need time to think it over.'

He looked at his watch. 'Five minutes?'

His confidence astonished her. 'Sit down, Monsieur Damala.'

'Please call me Aristide.'

'Then sit down, Aristide, and tell me whether you know anything at all about acting.'

'I know what it is like to play a part, to face a crowd when I feel like hiding in a corner, to say stupid things to people at parties who say stupid things to me. I have a good physique, a fine profile and an excellent speaking voice.'

'And a high opinion of yourself.'

'That is important too, isn't it, Sarah?'

For a moment she was silent, then spoke with seriousness. 'You have a certain outward visible appeal. But do you have inner qualities? An actor needs them too. Acting is not just the courage or conceit to stand up on a stage in front of people. It's something that comes from within. It's a will to communicate, a need to dominate. It's not for the sane. Most people are content, deeply grateful to be able to integrate one personality sufficiently to walk through life with it. An actor has a quite abnormal desire to assume many different personalities. It requires a facility nature gave to chameleons, not to people. It's a form of madness. But perhaps you have talents I haven't yet had an opportunity to appreciate.'

She had not intended to say so much. He appeared amused. When he spoke his voice was compromising. 'Perhaps the only talent I have is the one you appear to have heard about. But if it had proved fulfilling I would not be here now, nor listened when you said you would teach me.' He reached for her hand but she withdrew it.

'Yet you didn't come that afternoon,' she said.

He nodded. 'Later, I regretted it.'

She got up, crossed to a bureau and returned with the script of *Phèdre.* She sat down beside him. He moved close. 'We can read some lines together,' she said. 'This scene occurs between Phèdre and her stepson.' She felt his hand press her thigh and she said rather too earnestly: 'I am trying not to show my attraction to him but it is far too strong to hide.' She began reading: '"I am mad with love."'

'Would you repeat that?'

'"I am mad with love."' Her voice was pitched too high. 'Now you must speak the next line.'

'"Who is it that arouses you?"'

'No. It needs much more intensity. He really doesn't know that she loves him. Say it again.'

'Who is it that arouses you, Sarah?'

She ignored this and struggled on: '"Listen to me. Let all my madness speak. I love you. The gods have lit this flame within my soul. I cannot hide it. Have pity . . ."' His hand caressed her cheek. He took the script away and kissed her. It wasn't an eager kiss but it moved her. He drew back and looked at her with a childish innocence. 'What is it?' she asked.

'It is you, Sarah, who must have pity.' He seemed sad. 'I need you.'

She was touched. She reached out to him. They held one another close. Then they felt desire. 'Shall I send the carriage away?' he asked softly. For a moment she was tempted but thought it would be rash for him to stay. 'Not this time, Aristide,' she said. 'We shall meet tomorrow.'

When he had left she began thinking of the morning's rehearsals, of lunch with Jarrett and of the reception planned in her honour at Lady Dudley's. Aristide could be her escort to that. From now on she had someone to count on, to be at her side. No longer need she feel so vulnerable. She wasn't any more alone.

CHAPTER 15

London was to take Sarah to its heart and she would take London to hers. After the curtain fell on the first performance of *Phèdre* there were scenes of enthusiasm without precedent. But what the wildly cheering audience did not know was that the performance very nearly did not take place at all. For Sarah, as usual, had an attack of first-night nerves – 'not the stage-fright that paralyses but the kind that drives one wild', she said later. It also drove the company wild.

First she feared her pitch was wrong and a physician from the French Hospital was summoned to spray her throat. With five minutes to go she had trouble with her veil, her rings and her cameo belt, and blamed her dresser for having unpacked the stage wardrobe carelessly. When all seemed set she called for Jarrett and told him that she had forgotten her lines. Total loss of memory had set in. There was no possibility of a performance. He commiserated and suggested she should walk with him to the wings and look out on to the audience. It was one of the most elegant he had ever seen. There was no question of her going on, of course, but she should not deny herself the sight of the Royal Box in which sat the Duke of Connaught. Once she was in a position close to the stage he projected her on to it with a short, sharp shove, and at the sight of her the whole house rose. This gave her time to regain her self-possession. When she began her part she realized she had started in too high a pitch and as the play proceeded struggled to get it lower, a difficult feat for an actress as for a singer once in full flow. This battle for her vocal pitch combined with Phèdre's agony gave the effect of stark, horrible suffering. Her pleadings with Hippolytus, arms outstretched in cruel longing, were declaimed at such a peak of hysteria that the audience cringed. When the curtain fell she was lifted inanimate from the stage, but recovered in time to take her curtain calls.

'The exhausted actress,' said the *Daily Telegraph*, 'won her triumph only after tremendous physical exertion,' while the *Morning Post* raved over 'an exhibition marvellous in beauty of pose, in febrile force, in intensity and delivery'.

Sarah had proved herself to a public that had eagerly looked forward to her coming; it gave her great satisfaction. She had wanted to give them 'my very blood, my life, my soul', she had told Jarrett, and that was almost what she had given them. She had uttered no word of English. In the forty years of touring that lay ahead of her she would perform only in French. It was the style of her acting that captivated, unlike anything London had seen before.

Matthew Arnold described her as 'a fugitive vision of delicate features under a shower of hair and a cloud of lace'. Ellen Terry likened her to 'smoke from a burning paper'. To Wilde she was 'the incomparable one', to the painter Burne-Jones 'the supreme and glorious one'. There were no standards of comparison, only epithets to hint at a combination of the ethereal and the profoundly physical. 'Only her art could release her imprisoned energy,' said *The Times*, and they were right for theatre was her true reality. Not the stage but everyday life was a fantasy. But being a woman it was something she could not possibly admit to – or even realize.

Two days after their first London meeting Damala moved into Chester Square. Having a man about the house, and one who gave her such aesthetic and physical pleasure, completed her sense of well-being. The more she got to know London, the more it flattered her ego. English society did not normally accept stage people into its inner sanctums, but it was prepared to receive Sarah. She had come with some influential introductions. Even the Prince of Wales was interested in this *enfant terrible* from France. A fervent Francophile, he attended a performance on his return from Paris – and Sarah was indisputably *in.* The Churchills, the Dudleys, the Northrops, the Actons, the Cornwallises followed suit, not to mention the Rothschilds. When Sarah decided to send to France for some of her paintings and sculptures to mount a modest exhibition of them in London she felt fairly confident of some fashionable interest. What she did not anticipate was that no less than 1200 people would turn up to the opening or that the notables present would include Mr Gladstone. He even had a brief exchange of words with her.

'What moral lessons do you draw from *Phèdre*?' he asked.

Sarah thought hard; she had not anticipated so weighty a question. 'That we ought never to do what is irreparable?' she suggested.

'Then I take it you are against capital punishment?' he said.

'Yes,' Sarah promptly replied.

'Quite right.' The Grand Old Man of politics walked happily away; the next day he gave one of his most trenchant speeches on the subject to the House of Commons.

Wherever she went Sarah was impressed by the city's triumphant vitality. This was particularly evident on Sundays in Hyde Park, beloved by Londoners as a place of promenade. Women in bright silks and satins, flowered hats with veils of tulle and multi-coloured sunshades strolled with their men and children beside the flower beds. Along the bridle path at Rotten Row the lordly cantered on thoroughbreds and their children on Irish ponies. The park's roads were filled with dog-carts, open carriages and smart cabs, some with powdered footmen. Bands played to families in the tea gardens. She wrote home to Madame Guérard: 'To think that our wretched little President with his perverse bourgeois soul has been content to let our delightful Bois de Boulogne still bear traces of the injuries inflicted on it. How beautiful it used to be before the siege, with the young men caracoling in the Avenue des Acacias admired by every red-blooded Parisian.'

But as time went by Sarah forgot to compare London with Paris. She revelled in the vitality of a city in its golden age. The very future seemed to have come alive. It was a façade, of course, and beyond it was a maelstrom of injustice, squalor, crime, but it was a substantial one in this decade of imperial glory. Decline due to competition from America and Germany may already have set in but there was no visible sign of it. London was still the heart of the workshop of the world, the sounding board for ideas and new inventions. Sarah found the English character to her liking; it had a bland honesty that made up a lot for the lack of a Frenchman's style. The English liked her because she was a 'character', something they relish and admire. They were childlike in their enthusiasm for the riches that Empire and inventive skills had brought them, and she shared this thoroughly. She marvelled at their railway system that not only linked the capital with the country but was now burrowing beneath the city itself. She was impressed with the new powered lifts in the big hotels, the wonders of the typewriter, the first telephones and talk of airships. She realized that the coming electric age would revolutionize stage techniques. Everywhere there was an exuberant quest for more and more knowledge. It was personified in the great new museums going up in Kensington. The controversial fires lit by Darwin burned bright in private and public discussion and although Dickens still entertained and campaigned with his sagas of the masses there was about this Victorian England such vitality that Sarah vowed she would go back time and time again. 'Everywhere I go,' she wrote to Madame Guérard, 'I feel the love of life enveloping me.' And by now she was deeply in love herself.

With Aristide beside her she had visited the houses of the great. To the sophisticated the presence of so disconcertingly good-looking an escort ten years her junior gave added spice to her allure. She was the woman of the hour. Irving entertained them to lunch in his private dining-room at the Lyceum. Wilde gave them supper in Salisbury Street. Ellen Terry took them shopping. She gave poetry recitals at aristocratic houses. The Prince of Wales visited her dressing-room. And the only sour note came from Lady Frederick Cavendish, the martinet of society's *crème de la crème.* She strongly disapproved of 'a woman of notorious character' being fêted so ostentatiously. 'This woman is asked to respectable people's houses to act!' she thundered. 'It is an outrageous scandal!' But there was no risk of scandal now that she had Damala, someone whose presence gave her confidence and a shield. At first she had felt some guilt concerning Marie. But Marie appeared to accept the situation, continued to be a conscientious and reliable actress who never lacked for partners after theatre hours. Aristide seemed satisfied. Occasionally he reminded her of her promise, but seemed nevertheless to enjoy walking in her shadow.

At the end of each day, usually in the small hours of the morning, he was content, she thought, to know that she loved and needed him. His love-making was certainly virile, deft and lusty and proved that the ridiculous things that had been said about him were pure malice. This 'combination of Casanova and the Marquis de Sade' was often demanding but he was clearly devoted to her too. After making love to sleep enclosed by his warmth and awake to the beauty of his body gave her a deep sense of womanhood. It was as precious as the applause of an audience to whom she had given her best.

Aristide was a lover she felt guiltlessly able to indulge with presents. She supplied him with money and fine clothes; her reward was his youth, his charm, the gift of his body. In her unconventional reasoning that was a perfectly fair exchange. Animate beauty had always been far more interesting to her than objects. It was why she had spent so much on a menagerie and her choice of pets had been pioneeringly adventurous. Though she did not realize it Aristide was the most exotic so far, a languorous cat she left to sleep on in her bed when the duties of the day took her away from it, the hound-dog she joined there for relaxation.

The presence of this most fascinating of animals didn't dissuade her from acquiring others. She had heard about a zoo in Liverpool – Cross's Zoo – where lions might be bought. Having accumulated quite a lot of extra money from her recitals, painting and sculpture, she set her mind on buying one. She and Aristide took a train to Merseyside. They had trouble finding the place which was deep in dockland and less of a zoo than a compound for livestock brought by sea from Africa. The owner was not present but the travellers were directed to a backstreet tavern where a diminutive, bespectacled man was identified as Mr Cross.

He was enjoying a lunch-time pint of beer and had not expected to be waylaid at that moment by a shock-headed Frenchwoman and a young Greek. But he was entirely affable. 'Well,' said Sarah, after allowing him time to finish his drink. 'I want two lions today.' If she had spoken in English it would have sounded no less like a housewife's grocery list.

'Do you really, Madame,' said the friendly Cross. 'I'll show you what I have.'

They followed him back to the compound where he pointed to two huge lions in glowing health, their tails beating the air in savage ill-humour.

'New arrivals,' said Mr Cross.

To Aristide's relief she enquired if he had something

smaller. 'I want some young lions,' she said.

Mr Cross thought a while. He had, he said, tigers, leopards, jackals, pumas, cheetahs – and elephants.

'Dwarf elephants?' said Sarah.

Mr Cross shook his head. Aristide breathed relief.

But to Sarah it seemed the height of absurdity to have come all the way to Liverpool and go back empty-handed. She settled for a cheetah. 'It looks like a gargoyle on a castle of the Middle Ages,' she told Aristide.

Mr Cross then presented her, with the compliments of the house, with a chameleon. The fabulous little creature with its prehistoric look delighted her. Not only could it change colour but it could use its two lorgnette-like eyes independently – with its right eye it could look backward while its left looked ahead. 'The sort of vision you need for a career in the theatre,' she told Aristide.

Thus encumbered they took the return train, the cheetah caged in the guard's van and the chameleon fastened to a slender gold chain bought from a Liverpool jeweller. At St Pancras station they pacified a cabby with a substantial bribe and arrived ebulliently at Chester Square. From that moment until the time came for Sarah's return to Paris at summer's end her neighbours knew uneasily that at No. 77 there was a cheetah at the bottom of the garden!

Some French journalists had crossed the Channel to report Sarah's London season – *Figaro*, *Temps*, *Gil Blas* each had a correspondent there. They were watching her like hawks. While serious critics dealt fairly with her the journalists looking for sensational copy found plenty of material. Her liaison with 'the diplomatic Apollo' did not escape their notice. The lights at Chester Square sometimes burned through the night as Sarah and Aristide entertained. The parties noticeably mingled the upper crust with the frankly bohemian. They were quite aware that there had been complaints from more staid, less nocturnal residents.

But Sarah was enjoying life and wanted to live every minute. The mannered formal functions were one thing but to enjoy a city one had to mingle with the crowds. Only by slipping away with Aristide, who knew London, could she see its real night life, the taverns and supper rooms where chops and baked potatoes were mixed with entertainment that was often very obscene. With him she glimpsed the streets off the Haymarket crowded with brothels, the alleys of Soho, the clubs where notorious madames offered sexuality to suit all tastes. In order not to be recognized when they went to such quarters she on more than one occasion wore male attire. Aristide thought such escapades delightful, but when there arrived at Chester Square a letter from a men's tailor asking if she would wear a coat of his make he thought she should put a stop to it. *Figaro*'s man had filed a story and some Londoners read the Paris papers.

Nearly everything she did, and much that she did not do, was reported in their columns. At Madame Tussaud's she had spat in the face of the waxwork's likeness of her (in fact, she had admired it); at the Tower of London she had begged to be allowed to wear the crown jewels (she had asked politely if they could be handled); she had run into St James's Park naked (she had taken off her shoes one beautiful evening in Hyde Park); she had sent the Princess Royal an insulting letter (she had sent the Princess Royal roses to thank her for attending a performance); she wore no stays (she didn't).

But Sarah's life was so full that she seldom looked at the French newspapers, but Aristide, with time on his hands, had been reading them assiduously. The insinuations they made that he was being kept, that he was as much an extension of her bizarre image as the cheetah, pained him and paved the way for their first quarrel.

'I want to return to Paris,' he said one evening. She was

tired after a day of two performances. She thought he was teasing.

'In two months' time we'll all be going back,' she said. 'Then we'll see about getting you into something you can take an interest in. I think you would make a very handsome lawyer.'

'That is not what I want, Sarah,' he protested. 'It is not what we planned.'

She was alarmed. 'What is the matter?'

'I want to start rehearsing,' he said. His tone had been harsh but now it became offensive. 'Don't look so surprised. It was your suggestion, remember? "I will teach you how to act."' He mimicked her mannerisms. 'We were dancing at the time you first said it. It was your special evening. The champagne flowed. There were toasts to our divine Sarah . . .'

He had been drinking, she realized, and at once began to placate him. 'You've had a lonely evening. I should have been more thoughtful. You could have come to the theatre. You know how I hate leaving you here.'

He mimicked her again. '"I will tell you all about acting."' He reached for a decanter and poured himself a brandy. 'But divine Sarah forgot her promise. It wasn't convenient, was it?'

'Why didn't you come to the theatre?' she asked quietly. Her mind was now quite alert and she felt very concerned.

'Because I hate the kind of looks I get. They know, you see, that I'm Sarah's Greek, the stud she keeps in a cage – along with the rest of her menagerie.'

She had never seen him like this; once or twice at parties she had thought he drank too freely but he had seemed so happy to be involved with her.

'Tomorrow,' she said, 'I will speak to Jarrett. I have been selfish. I thought that being important to me, so essential to my life . . .'

'No, Sarah.' His tone was stony. 'No one is really essential to you. I want the chance you offered.'

'I will see Jarrett in the morning,' she repeated. 'I'm very tired now.' She got up to leave. Three months of happiness hadn't prepared her for this. 'Good night, Aristide.'

'By the way,' he said as she was leaving the room. 'I saw Marie this afternoon.' She froze. 'Don't worry. I ran into her in a pharmacy. She has been having headaches. That's why she missed the afternoon performance. You work that girl too hard.'

'Yes,' she said. 'We used her understudy.'

In her bedroom she realized she was exhausted. She wanted to cry. She got into bed and lay there sleeplessly. An hour must have passed before she heard his footsteps. He undressed unsteadily, climbed into bed but faced away from her. But after a while he turned and wrapped her in his arms.

Rehearsals were about to begin for *The Lady of the Camelias* and Sarah suggested to Jarrett that Aristide should be given the role of Armand. The impresario thought she was joking but then the seriousness of the problem dawned – he was dealing with a woman in love. Her critical factors had flown.

Jarrett had no ill-will for Damala; he saw him as a stabilizing influence upon Sarah. Up to now she had shown very little of the famous temperament. He had put this down to the fact that she was happy. But that she considered a professional career for her young Greek was a total surprise. Experience told him not to say that the idea was preposterous. Instead he agreed to hear him read.

The scene chosen for Damala's audition was the one in which Armand tries to convince Marguerite that his love for her is not a fly-by-night emotion. 'You are mad, Marguerite. I love you! I am not saying that you are pretty or that you will please me for three or four months. I am saying that you are all my soul! All my hopes! All my life! I love you! What more can I say to you?'

What indeed! Strongly emotive stuff but critical to the play's credibility. By means of it Armand must convince the irresolute Marguerite, who has heard infatuation's voice before, that his love is deep, sincere and reliable enough for her to resolve to make a good woman of herself.

On the morning of the audition Aristide got up from the concubinal bed at the same time as Sarah. At breakfast she was full of solicitous advice.

'At a reading one should never try to give everything of oneself – contrive rather to *suggest* a potential power,' she told him. 'On an undressed stage in an empty theatre performance is not called for. In fact, it is impossible. You must underplay your speeches, convince the few who are there that once surrounded by all the effects, the furniture, the lighting, the intelligence you are showing will reveal itself as true acting power.'

'I know all that,' he said. 'Don't go on or you'll make me nervous.'

But it was Sarah who was nervous.

'You should wear the corn-flower blue suit, and that deep blue shirt from Revelle's,' she advised. 'When you get to the theatre spend a little time with the man who dresses Angelo – and with the hairdresser too.'

'How does Angelo feel about me?'

'What do you mean?'

'About my taking over his part.'

'We'll see,' she said nervously. 'Darling, I want you to show yourself at your very best today. I'm really very concerned for you. I remember how I felt years ago at the Comédie. I went there without a partner to feed my lines. I didn't know you were expected to have one. And I recited a fable of La Fontaine. I was only seventeen.'

Aristide looked bored. He took a cigarette from the gold case she had given him, looked at his watch and said they ought to be leaving. In the hall she waited for a kiss. It seemed important on such a morning. But he had paused to examine himself, peering closely into the mirror to pay particular attention to his eyes. 'I've put on ten years since meeting you,' he said.

She laughed uneasily. 'Promise me, Aristide, that you will not be nervous. I want them to see how right I am about my protégé.'

Before leaving he gave her a pert, indulgent kiss. As they climbed into her carriage he hugged her briefly and grinned. 'I'll make an absolute fool of myself,' he said.

On stage he certainly looked the part, a romantically handsome Armand. Far from being nervous he was in fact too self-assured. The effect was to dominate the scene instead of giving it to Marguerite as is essential to its poignancy. His timing was haphazard. His French with its Greek pronunciation which Sarah liked so much jarred when projected from a stage. Nevertheless, she looked on admiring as he pursued a tortuous course through the sickly phraseology. There was nothing that in time couldn't be rectified, she thought. And he was so good-looking. 'Isn't he beautiful?' she remarked to Jarrett.

'Not when he tries to act,' he replied. It seemed a time for honesty.

'Nonsense. I'm surprised at you. His gestures are a little stilted, I agree, but I can smooth them down.'

Jarrett was incredulous. 'You can't be planning to put him on stage! You'll be the laughing stock of London.'

This annoyed her. 'I'm not planning to put him on in London. I'll break him in when we go to Brighton. Then he'll be ready for London on our return.'

Jarrett felt that time might be on his side. Some way would have to be found of bringing Sarah back to earth. Damala could be the ruin of them all.

'You were marvellous,' she told Aristide that evening,

'but you need time to perfect certain things. Technique has to be learned and that means work – and perhaps some disappointment.'

She wanted to tell him that an actor is a very special breed. If he is not shaken by anger, if pity does not move him he will appear insipid. An audience will remember that it is at a play, that an artificial hero is in front of it. An audience that goes home unmoved by the performance of an actor, that has received no artistic pleasure, will rightly feel cheated. 'It is a very sensitive craft,' she said simply.

'You make it sound so mysterious,' he said with impatience. 'Times have changed, Sarah. In your student days acting was considered as something to be learnt like any other subject. But you've told me how old-fashioned were the attitudes at the Conservatoire and the Comédie. Today acting is more naturalistic. Surely you don't want me to become an acting *student*. You said yourself I have a natural talent.'

'The trend is *towards* realism,' she said. (It was she, in fact, who had influenced it that way.) 'It's still a craft that has to be painstakingly learned. No amount of talent can relieve us of that.'

'You mean I am not ready to play Armand.'

'I have told Jarrett you will play the role in Brighton.'

'Why not in London?'

'Because you are not quite ready.'

'You have no faith in me.'

'That's not true.'

'It must be the reason, Sarah,' he insisted. 'You are ten years behind the times. I'm not aspiring to be a tragedian. Nothing so heavy. I've got all that it takes to be a light romantic actor. You said so yourself. Or is it that you're getting bored with me?'

'You're being stupid.' She was feeling the strain. There was so much he didn't understand. An actor worthy of the name must be capable of a continuous dissection of personality. He should be able to suffer the remorse of Macbeth, to feel the savage love of Phèdre, to fall in love at first sight as Romeo did, to weep with Juliet. Hamlet's frenzy will make the audience shudder only if the actor really is and feels like Hamlet. It was a delusion for an actor to think that he could wear the vestment of another's soul while preserving his own, create an artificial exterior while maintaining his ordinary feelings intact. An actor could not divide his personality between himself and his part; he was obliged to lose his ego during the time he remained on the stage, let his consciousness skip from age to age, from one race to another, from one social level to another, from hero to villain. Acting, she wanted to tell him, is a crushing burden, an almost superhuman thing if it is to be accomplished in all its fullness and be worthy of the name of art. But all she said was: 'Looks are not enough, Aristide.'

He was angry. 'Very well, I'll wait for Brighton. But in the meantime I want a little amusement. I'm getting rather tired of being in a cage.'

'It's getting late,' she said sadly.

That night she waited for his footsteps but fell asleep alone.

When she awoke to the realization that he was not beside her she was frightened and self-accusatory. She wanted to make amends. But where was he and with whom? While she strove to adjust her mind to the commitments of the day a thought kept recurring – was he with Marie? Had she driven him back to her for consolation? The possibility that he had decided to return to France was more bearable. She had other disturbing thoughts. His heavy drinking had begun to cause her concern. At times of listlessness he took cognac far too freely. Was he taking other drugs too? He made regular, unexplained visits to pharmacies. Like herself he was highly strung, elated one day, grounded in lacklustre the next, but at times the degree of his elation was unnatural. His energy at times was so boundless that in shedding it something of himself was consumed. Being hypersensitive, she told herself guiltily, he was capable of over-reacting to slights or misunderstandings. Had he left the house believing she had no faith in him? Was he in some shadow world in this huge impersonal city unconscious, drugged, dying? With each minute her fears and fantasies multiplied as she conjured scenes of lurid tragedy. Guilt helped her weave them. She felt herself to be at fault. All she could do was to wait and hope that a knowledge of her love and need for him would bring him safely back.

He came into the bedroom just as she had started to dress. He closed the door and stared at her. The sunlight of the August morning vivified his features, heightening their deep Latin tone. His face was rough and unshaven, his hair tousled. She had never seen his eyes so bright. He looked wild, burdened with imprisoned strength. He walked over to her. Holding her firmly he stripped her of her negligée. Then he lifted her and carried her to the bed. Impatiently he shed his own clothes and stood before her. He pulled her head forward and pressed it to his genitals to instil her with knowledge of the power there. Then he mounted her, forcing her to accept with such abruptness that the pain of it caused her to cry out. He thrust and withdrew, penetrating and withdrawing again and again to repeat the shock of it. With his mouth he explored her neck, her shoulders, and bit into her flesh. Previously, darkness had hidden her faint scars but now in the light he discovered them and these he branded too so that they burned into her memory again. Arriving at his climax he lay still for a moment before moving inside her again, thrusting deeper, each time deeper, until she no longer felt a sense of selfness; her flesh became his flesh in the ordeal. When he had finished he fell back, nestling beside her with the limpness of a sleepy child. Only when he slept did she notice that on the inside of his arms were numerous marks, some as neat as pinpricks, others quite bad scars, and she knew with dismay that what she had suspected was in fact true: he was a morphine addict.

CHAPTER 16

To a more conventional woman the discovery of Damala's addiction would have brought despair. It kindled pity in Sarah. Was she sexually obsessed? She believed that she loved him. Love, not lust, was what she had looked for and when in time his weakness and excesses denied her intimacy with him she would mourn the loss of something more important than sexuality, more profound than joy. She would grieve for his failure as a man – and blame herself for it. But for the moment, she had only one course in mind. Damala must marry her.

Marriage seemed the only way to hold him and by holding him give herself time to make him sound and healthy. It was to be her first bow to the gods of convention and would prove a tragic folly. Certainly she feared infidelity, but her belief that the bonds of matrimony would be a defence against it showed how far her reason had strayed. In later years she would rationalize the marriage as an act of love dictated by a devious fate ('God,' she would say, 'writes straight on crooked lines') and recall Damala as the only true love of her life – even though he came close to wrecking it. At no time would she admit that he was unworthy, and she would be loyal to the end.

The London first night of *The Lady of the Camelias* saw more scenes of acclaim. Damala had said he would be there but after the performance he did not join her in the dressing-room. He had attended most of the rehearsals in anticipation of his own debut in Brighton. Each evening she had coached him and he had made progress. She believed that with herself on stage beside him he would be a convincing Armand. She never expected or wanted star performances from her leading men. Damala would make up in physical appeal what he lacked in experience and technique. She sincerely believed he would prove his detractors wrong, and there were many in the company who, like Jarrett, resented her plan to use him.

They had lived on a calmer plain since the night of his absence. As though atoning for his unfeeling treatment of her he had been unusually considerate. She had even been able to reveal her concern but his denial of an addiction had seemed plausible in the light of his relaxed and thoughtful manner. For a week she had lived in hope and had done her utmost to give him confidence. When he did not come to the dressing-room she was concerned.

She changed quickly from her costume and hurried to the stage door. A crowd had gathered but she pushed through them to reach her carriage. She told the coachman to drive with speed to Chester Square.

On arrival she found Jarrett already there full of good humour, delighted by the continuing success of the London season. The box-office receipts were a record. He had future plans for her – a return visit to London followed by a tour in America. He also wanted to remind her that in the morning she was expected at the Admiralty where the First Lord and other naval dignitaries were to entertain her. But she paid him scant attention. She had seen Damala at the top of the stairs. He had a glass in his hand. Jarrett left. 'Where were you tonight?' she asked, once they were alone. 'You told me you would be at the theatre.'

'I was there,' he said, 'but only for the first act.' His manner was one of child-like pique. 'It was bad enough watching Angelo in my role. I rehearse and rehearse and he gets the acclaim.'

'I've told you that you will play the part at Brighton. It isn't so long to wait. I'm hurt that you didn't stay. I took eleven calls. Where did you go?'

'Nowhere in particular.'

Suddenly she was angry. 'Were you with Marie?'

He snapped back at her. 'I will not be questioned, Sarah. I am not part of the menagerie. Out of your sight for an hour and I'm assumed to be on the prowl.'

'It isn't an assumption I like to make,' she told him, 'but you have the reputation of a puma. Isn't what we are trying to do worth some discipline? I'm putting you on at Brighton against opposition. Can't you see how worried I am? Temperament from you at this time doesn't help.'

'If I were allowed to act, to feel I was getting somewhere, your puma could be caged.'

'Then marry me, Aristide.'

He was stunned.

'I mean it. We'll get the necessary papers tomorrow and be married before the end of the week.'

For a moment he was silent. 'All right, Sarah, we'll get married, but we can't do much tomorrow.'

'Why?'

'You can't let the Navy down!' They both smiled.

They plunged into marriage four days later. Nominally she was a Roman Catholic, he of the Greek Orthodox Church. But the clergy of the Protestant church they chose, St Andrew's of Wells Street, had no qualms. In return for a sizeable contribution to the funds an unpretentious ceremony made them man and wife. Sarah then hurried back to the theatre to tell Jarrett that she was married and intended to make her husband a fully-fledged acting member of the company. If there were objections she would return with him to Paris. Aware that he was beaten, Jarrett agreed to Damala's debut. He viewed the thought of Brighton with a heavy heart; the greatest actress he had ever presented was risking her career for the sake of an amateur.

If Sarah thought that by launching Damala at Brighton he would be sheltered from critical comment she was wrong. The Theatre Royal there, a stone's throw from the fantastic Pavilion the Prince Regent had built a century earlier, was by no means a backwoods theatre. Its audiences were composed of well-to-do sophisticates, many of them emigrés from London, who regarded their coastal city of Georgian squares and colonnaded terraces as the last retreat of dignity and good taste. These qualities they believed were fast disappearing from the capital with its thrusting new middle class. Since the Regency had made Brighton fashionable its theatres had been able to attract the greatest names – the Keans, Edmund and Charles, Joseph Grimaldi, William Macready and another famous Sarah – Mrs Sarah Siddons, the 'Queen of Tragedy'. They had all played at the Theatre Royal. The theatre was now under the direction of Mrs Ellen Chart, a highly talented actress who had inherited it on the death of her husband. She had refurbished it and equipped it with electric lighting. Under her management it was enjoying immense prestige. Brightonians believed that what Brighton liked first, London subsequently applauded. So when they received a production the capital had priorly acclaimed they were ready to pounce. It was an audience apt to see itself as a giant-killer.

To this repository of recalcitrance the newly-weds travelled in style – a private coach was supplied with the compliments of the London to Brighton Railway – and they were quite unaware that most of London's theatre critics and a sprinkling of French correspondents were further down the train.

From the outset Damala was regarded as an extension of his wife's eccentricity. He was never taken seriously as an actor. The journalists who interviewed him at their hotel before the performance believed that through him they could identify more closely with Sarah and discover what life with her was like. Was it true that she bathed in goat's milk? Had the Prince of Wales been to Chester Square? To be treated merely as a funnel for this kind of information, which doubtless they would exaggerate, was demeaning. He wanted to talk about himself but he had become 'Monsieur Sarah Bernhardt' – and it infuriated him.

Nor did this improve relations with Sarah. They were to deteriorate further when he read his notices for inevitably he gained no laurels while she received great praise. But even if he had been a better actor the hapless Greek would have suffered much the same fate. The play was dominated first to last by her towering talent. With her on the stage no audience was capable of appreciating another player. Her authority and extraordinary mystique held it captive. She could sway it this way and that. Against her subtly changing humours no one stood much chance. Even the most experienced critics had to *will* themselves as an act of professional discipline to attend other performances, should they be inclined, and on this occasion they were so inclined because of Damala's connection with Sarah. But apart from some touching moments in the final act, wrought from him by her astonishing power, he was undistinguished. 'In time and with a great deal of work,' wrote the *Brighton Herald*'s man, 'the actor who played Armand will, we hope, become a much better match for his teacher. No young actor could wish for a better one.' And that was one of the kindest of the notices.

'Who pays these scavengers to write this rubbish?' he asked savagely after he had read the notices at Chester Square.

'Don't read them,' she said protectively.

'"The biggest tragedy of the evening was Mr Bernhardt's performance."' He read this one aloud to her.

'That is beneath contempt,' she said.

'"Let us hope that exposure to his wife will help him gain some of her talent"! But they all praise you.'

'Stop torturing yourself, Aristide. Every one of us has been through this. I can remember word for word my first notice. It followed a performance at the Comédie – "Mademoiselle Bernhardt carries herself well and pronounces with perfect precision. That is all that can be said about her at the moment."'

She laughed at the memory hoping he too would see the irony. But he was obsessed with resentment at the treatment he had received.

'I am simply curious to know how much the people who hate me pay the Press to write this stuff. Isn't it obvious that members of your own company are jealous of my relationship with you? What could be simpler than to slip them a sovereign in return for discrediting me? Jarrett, you know, can't stand the sight of me.'

'We all start our careers like this, Aristide,' she said seriously. 'It's a world of cruel knocks and strains. Many of the critics are themselves thwarted actors. It's never possible to please them all. I gave up reading reviews years ago. Be content that you've begun. Your feet are on the ladder. You can become a fine actor, but you must work. Years from now you'll look back and wonder why you were so hurt by these people who make a living out of us. You may come to think they weren't worth the heart-break – or even perhaps that they were not as unfair as you think now. It's not a profession for the over-sensitive. An actor has got to be thick-skinned. Be patient.'

'Then you think these parasites are right.'

Sadly she watched him leave. Jarrett had been right when he warned that by encouraging Damala she was risking his pride and perhaps her own career. Where would it all end? She heard the street door close. His footsteps moved across the square. Suddenly she was homesick. London, which had given her so much pleasure, was a foreign city again. She was very, very tired.

'I hate these tall London houses,' she wrote to Madame Guérard that evening. 'Their windows only open half-way, the top half or the bottom half. One may even have the pleasure of opening them a little at the bottom and a little at the top, but not at all in the middle. They go up or down but never outward. Nothing marks more clearly the difference in the character of the two nations. Ours open wide, the sun enters, the air sweeps away the confusion of our minds. They shut in the same way, as simply as they open. Here the windows keep their selfish, perfidious character showing us the same low sky, the same funereal gloom. Sometimes I want to break them open just to feel free . . .'

It was time to go home.

CHAPTER 17

'Cannibals!' Sarah shouted when she had read the newspaper articles Madame Guérard had assiduously but unhappily saved for her. 'Has this filth been appearing all the time I've been in England? I've never read anything so despicable!' There was worse to come. Mam'selle felt bound to show her the slim volume that had become a best-seller. At every bookstall in Paris *The Memoirs of Sarah Barnum* was on display and it was the most invidious attack to date.

Barnum and Bailey's circus, which had opened in Brooklyn in 1871 as 'the greatest show on earth', was already a byword for voracious self-advertisement, but that was only pertinent to the pamphleteer's choice of title. It depicted Sarah Barnum as an actress with an insatiable appetite for publicity who would stoop to immoral means to achieve it. The scurrilous work portrayed a depraved and vicious monster, a woman who had climbed to fame and power by blackmail, corruption and a licentious sexual life. The title left no doubt as to whom the leading character was supposed to be. And this dark parody of Sarah's life also involved Judith, Aunt Rosine, Prince Henri, Madame Guérard and even Maurice in hideously distorted caricature. Lewdly illustrated, it was also pornographic and anti-Semitic, a vicious lampoon designed to crucify. The newspaper articles, from provincial as well as Parisian journals and variously dated, accused her of having lived a flagrantly immoral life in London culminating in a marriage to a Greek gigolo who, it was implied, was a mere decoy for her deviations into transvestism and lesbianism. The allegation that she had been nude when she received the Prince of

Wales in her dressing-room seemed tame by comparison.

What a homecoming! At the Gare du Nord there had been no welcoming crowd. Now she knew why. Madame Guérard had met her bringing Maurice, who was noticeably taller and wearing his first knickerbocker suit. But it had been a harrowing journey. Damala had spent it in the cabin of a pretty English ingénue whom she had recruited in London believing the girl to have a good future. But Damala had infatuated her and he had encouraged her quite irresponsibly to return with them to Paris. Since his failure to impress as an actor, for which he held Sarah responsible, he had become increasingly spiteful. The last week in London had been torture. He cared no longer, it seemed, to hide his weaknesses from her. When sober his manner was cynical and sardonic but she had seen little of him. She knew that he was increasing his drug intake. He had used the morphine needle even in their bedroom. Arguments developed, bitterly accusatory, and she was torn between pity and despair. She had destroyed his pride, his sense of identity, he said. She had lashed back with denunciations of his promiscuity. Every quarrel ended with his departure from the house, leaving her in utter misery.

Finding herself alone on the day they were due to leave she had prayed for the first time since her convent days. It had calmed her. She had married a sick man and she resolved to live with the problem. Damala had never promised fidelity. She had refused to admit to his weaknesses. The marriage had been of her devising.

He returned in time for the journey and in an equable frame of mind and she determined there would be no more arguments.

But now this – this savagery in print! 'Who could have been so malicious?' she asked.

'We have found out,' Mam'selle replied sadly. 'It was Marie Colombier.'

Damala had lain sprawled on Sarah's couch since their

arrival. Now he watched her with wry humour.

He had found her home to be as showily theatrical and gaudily feminine as he had expected. From its ornate ceilings to its cluttered mantels it proclaimed her. It smelled of her. From every angle abstractions oppressed him, the annotated programmes mounted in frames, the Mucha posters, the sculpted head, portraits in oils, photographs with friends. The weight of all this was overpowering. It excluded him. Her son, as mother-fixated as any boy could be, clearly did not like him. As for the forlorn creature in institutional black she called Mam'selle, he thought her to be the wife of the concierge. But she shared Sarah's every confidence, a trusted soul, an accessory. He had needed a drink. Fortunately that was not in short supply. The fine cognac made him feel better as he listened to Sarah's ravings with keen irony. Hadn't she told him not to be disturbed by journalistic bilge? Marie had certainly put the cat among the pigeons!

'What are you complaining about?' he asked her tauntingly. 'Your name is on everyone's lips.'

'Mama,' put in Maurice, 'are you bald? It says in one of the papers that you wear a wig. And did you smoke cigars on the balcony of your house in London? It says you did.'

Sarah could contain herself no longer. 'I'll kill her,' she said. 'I took her to England even though she cannot act. She's never been able to. She's repaid me with treason. Well, she won't get away with it. I'm going to thrash her within an inch of her life.'

The caged birds fluttered, a pet dog cowered as, bowed down by concern, Mam'selle followed her from the room.

Damala stretched himself. He sipped his cognac and gave Maurice a friendly wink. The boy looked sheepish. Then Mam'selle returned. 'She's gone to Marie Colombier's,' she said, 'and she's carrying a riding-whip!'

Not only had Sarah taken a riding-crop : she had 'armed'

herself with a stage dagger, and was on her way to the Rue de Thann to Marie's tiny top-floor flat. At the sight of her Marie fled. Thwarted, Sarah set about wrecking the place, slashing cushions, smashing mirrors, pulling pictures off the wall, breaking furniture and hurling knick-knacks into the fire. When all her passion was spent the place looked as if it had been shelled. When Marie returned to it she thought the wreckage resembled 'something out of those ancient stories of devil worshippers, and their vengeance upon the holy', an understandably appalled if self-righteous reaction to the saturnalian disorder. And symbolically, atop the litter of broken porcelain and savaged upholstery, lay a photograph of Damala, its frame smashed but its inscription still bright – 'to my little pigeon of the rooftops'.

Shaken but resilient the pigeon now flew to the offices of the more important newspapers. She invited each to send a representative to inspect the destruction at her flat. The next day it was headline news. Marie's book was in even greater demand. Nothing could have convinced the public more that the portrait drawn in 'Sarah Barnum' was close to the facts of life. Sarah had damned herself and the sales of the book soared even higher.

On her return to Paris she had expected to be hugely in demand. It was a cruel blow to find herself in such disrepute. The furore over the book continued. There were editorials, petitions from women's groups and statements from the churches, and all were critical. It had become a national debate. She was a classic case of over-exposure. Publicity, that powerful genie she had so assiduously cultivated, had become an ogre. It was fast ruining her. In vain she sought producers and managers and performers, many of them old friends, to convince them that she was still quite sane, to win their understanding, and while most were affable, many made a joke of it, others sympathized, it seemed that over the entire profession had settled the conviction that she was dangerous. The theatrical establishment joined ranks in a tacit unspoken agreement. Sarah was too hot to handle. As if that were not enough, there arrived from Montigny a claim for damages for having broken her contract and gone to London.

Meanwhile Damala was spending her money as liberally as if it were his own, which it was under the laws governing marriage. When not absent he loafed about the house to everyone's unease. He took morphine heavily. The effect was to create a split personality, elated on some days, dulled and incapacitated on others. His sexual adventures also came close to home. There was evidence for Sarah to come across, letters from infatuated girls left open and probably unread. The police had made cursory enquiries about a prostitute who had been raped and left unpaid.

Yet there were times when he seemed to resurrect from this tangle and waste some semblance of the man she had once thought beautiful, an hour at twilight perhaps, when she came upon him in their bedroom where he had slept the day away, the light of evening touching his sleeping body and bathing him in innocence. Sometimes she would lie on the bed beside him, feeling a devastating pity, recalling past rapture helplessly. But if he awoke her presence seemed to annoy him. She would leave him. Later, he would depart from the house as on the night before. Still she believed that she had failed him, that she had been inadequate to meet his need. A stronger love, she told herself, might have cured him.

Madame Guérard, too, was feeling the strain. Maurice was now at boarding school, safe from the neuroses of the household. This made her feel that perhaps her duty was done. She was never happy when Damala was around. His mounting dependence made him careless – things got broken, emptied phials of his narcotic were left about, he was lax about clothes and cleanliness. Once she found him in Sarah's bedroom nude and so weak from vomiting that a doctor had to be called. Madame Guérard was by now in her sixties, not physically robust and rather deaf. She could not avoid overhearing the bitter quarrels of the star-crossed pair and felt torn between loyalty to Sarah and her need to remove herself from such distress. She even felt pity for Damala but it was tempered by resentment of the disastrous turn in Sarah's fortunes. She stayed in the belief that catastrophe was near.

Loyal, too, was Victorien Sardou. He intervened with Montigny to dissuade him from the law suit but failed to find her work. One evening they met at the Café Roussel in a little side street close to the Odéon where so many years before they had talked about the theatre before either had made a name in it. 'I spoke to Montigny,' Sardou reported, 'and he will withdraw proceedings. But he's still bitter although deep down he has affection for you. He's firm about one thing – he will never work with you again.'

'He was my last hope,' she said. 'I've tried everyone. No one will engage me. They think I'm a public menace, that audiences would come to destroy me. I am a national insult. The Third Republic has done so little. Alsace and Lorraine are symbols of the pride we lost in the war. I've been made a scapegoat. Yet how quickly the public forgets. I've always been a patriot, Victorien, but not the kind that waves flags. I've tried to express what I feel in my work and with my hands, these hands that nursed the wounded and scrubbed the floors of latrines. Now I'm ridiculed as a Jewess who vulgarized France when abroad. What is it that makes Paris so capricious?'

'They hate as forcefully as they love,' said Sardou. 'What will you do?'

'I don't know,' she replied. 'For the first time in my life I really don't know.'

But Sarah still did not realize how completely she had been rejected. She resolved to give a dinner party to which she would invite thirty guests selected from the artistic and political life of Paris. She had been on friendly terms with all of them. In defiance of her worsening finances she decided on a lavish affair. She would preside in a throne-like chair over a table weighted down with silver plate. But one by one answers came from private secretaries with requests to be excused. Sarah ruefully learnt that most of these leaders of Paris life would be out of town or had prior commitments. Two days before the planned occasion she cancelled it, and with a heavy heart faced the fact that her ostracism was complete.

Something else occurred to bring home the hostility that had developed around her. Because it symbolized public feeling it was more hurtful even than the cold shoulder of power. One morning a small group loitered at the gates to her house. Someone threw a stone as she got into her carriage. Hatred from a stranger seemed the final judgement, as positive a verdict as a tossed bouquet. The mindlessness of this violence sickened her and as the days passed she lost her zestful energy and with it the will to work.

Damala's life-style precluded any possibility that he might be of help. He was not aware that she was in a serious position. To him she had always represented success, the ability to adapt. He took her resourcefulness for granted and there had been no apparent change in her living standards. When he was in the house, aloof, fractious, churlish, she still regarded him as her responsibility. His needs were simple if costly. They were being supplied in as controlled a manner as possible for now she knew there was no cure. Brandy by day, morphine at nightfall. After a rally of energy he would leave the house with a buoyant air only to return a shadow of a man haunted by an inexpressible guilt. All he needed then was further brandy to soothe him into sleep. She felt overwhelming sorrow for him, realizing that he too had spun dreams he had no gift to realize. The one advantage life had provided was diminishing as his body coarsened and lost its litheness. But as her material concerns perplexed her she was sometimes intolerant. The nature of his malady led to deceptions – money disappeared, small possessions were taken away and sold, responsibility for the thefts was placed with cunning plausibility on the servants. The climax came when Sarah received from a jeweller bills that sent her finances hurtling deeper into the red. From Cartier a golden owl set in rubies. From Van Cleef a string of graduated pearls – purchases that had not been made for her.

Finding him sufficiently lucid she asked him why.

'You have put me in chains,' he said. 'You created a puppet. And I have no money of my own.'

'But these presents were to other women. Doesn't that seem very cruel? I have no work. Nobody will employ me.'

'Sarah out of favour?' It was not to be believed. 'It's only temporary, my dear. You're like a sponge – you soak up what's around you and you float. You'll make a comeback. You'll never lack for money. Sarah Barnum's indestructible – it's the others who get destroyed.'

His hatred appeared to sober him. For a moment she saw the man whose independence and self-esteem had once so intrigued her.

'I have done nothing but love you,' she said. 'I have never loved anyone else.'

'Are you asking for gratitude? When you have everything it's easy to give. You have never known what suffering is, Sarah. You've been spoiled by success. Bouquets and compliments have blinded you to what life is about. Applause is all the love you really need and by ruthlessness you'll get it again. I hope it will be more satisfying. You'll still live in a world apart. The common touch will elude you. You will see a face in a crowd that excites you and you will envy it its pride. But as you get older the ability to possess people will get harder. You are going to be a very lonely woman.'

There was nothing more to be said. His vicious diatribe had exhausted both of them. Suddenly he rose and snatched the bills away. 'I'll take them,' he said. 'I won't be indebted any longer. I prefer my freedom.'

She heard the street door close. In the garden a dog was barking, an incessant pointless protest at the futility of things. Her life was at its lowest ebb.

CHAPTER 18

Damala's absences had become such an accepted part of the household's haphazard life-style that it was some time before it occurred to Sarah to wonder whether from this one he would return at all. The days passed uncounted as she brooded over the degree of his bitterness. The savageness of it had numbed her.

Then it began to feed her sense of guilt. Despite present setbacks was she privileged above the common run of people? Had she been shielded from the harsher realities? The possibility that his accusations might be based on envy did not occur to her. They were so very intimidating.

It was true that she felt the gods had blessed her – or cursed her – with secret, hidden fires, but she had accepted her talent with humility. It was true that she had guarded it with aggression but she had always thought of it as something to be shared. Only by sharing it with the public was it truly realizable, which was why she felt impotent when not allowed to work.

Did the average person have any hint of perception of just how much heartbreak, sacrifice and self-discipline went into a creative performance? The torture of self-doubt, the battle against feelings of futility, the loneliness and fear of failure? The majority journeyed through a terrain of unrealizable dreams with no chance at all of treading the heights, and the obverse side of adulation was always envy. It could so easily be turned inside out. Yet it was to their grey country that she had striven to bring enchantment. This giving had been her bond with them. But Damala's condemnation had clouded her vision of it.

As time went on and he did not return, her anxieties

blended with a more practical, immediate concern, the need to reduce her overheads. She was facing financial ruin.

The first to go was her houseboy who had been with her for six years. Now in his early twenties, Emile offered to work for no wages but she found him employment with Sardou on the understanding that he would be re-engaged should her fortunes improve. One by one the staff were relinquished and this was followed by the sale of the two bays and the more exotic animals in the menagerie. To clear debts run up by Damala she sold jewellery, paintings and bric-à-brac. Still she could not make ends meet. It was not in her character to write begging letters, but she wrote a letter to Alfonse de Rothschild charmingly couched in bravado which suggested that he purchase a bronze head of her because she had grown tired of it. De Rothschild responded with a cheque for a sum in excess of what she had asked but she returned a third of it to him saying that the price she had named was what she had wanted. She was still the proud mixture of practicality and impulse, but now it was a conscious act. Her spirit was nearly broken.

Damala had left in January and now it was early spring but she was immune to its restorative powers. Weeks passed in a preoccupation with survival.

The most important asset left was the lease to her home and its value had greatly increased. Now she saw no alternative to selling. She would find a small villa outside Paris with room for Maurice when he was home from school. Once installed she and Mam'selle would find work such as dressmaking for the wives of the bourgeoisie who would remember her and be intrigued to have Bernhardt as their dressmaker. Later she would write her memoirs which in time might prove a profitable means to vindication. She was only thirty-five and had already lived more abundantly than most of her generation. Before deciding finally on this course she had something else in mind which she felt somehow impelled to explore.

On a morning in late April she set out on a nostalgic journey to Versailles, for she wanted to see the Grand-Champ Convent again. It was as if voices from the past were calling and, in particular, she had been thinking of Mother St Sophie. As the train pulled out of Paris through the sprawling new suburbs she recalled her first journey all those years before. She had travelled then by diligence with her mother and Aunt Rosine and had seen her mother's house get smaller as the coach drew away. She remembered having hidden her tears in a blue silk muffler before falling asleep to rouse only when they arrived. Then her luggage was put on the pavement, the little metal trunk, a case of games and a kite given to her by her mother's concierge. Jumping down from the diligence she had looked with apprehension at the great gateway surmounted by a stone cross. Through the iron railings she had seen the barrack-like convent, three storeys of damp grey stone. Yet, she now recalled, that prison had freed her of elementary fears. It had offered her a life that she would have embraced with eagerness had the theatre not intervened. Was it calling her back to that vocation?

On arrival at Versailles station she walked to the convent feeling more confident with each step that the journey had significance. Something or someone awaited her there with a message. It would give her a sense of direction. Whatever or whoever it was had been there all the time waiting for the moment to confide.

The courtyard, which she remembered as huge and awesome, seemed smaller and more ordinary but children stared from the same forlorn windows. In the entrance hall she asked a shy young nun if she might see the Mother Superior, explaining that she had once been a pupil there. She was shown into the waiting-room which was exactly as she remembered it. The shining polished floor, the hard wooden benches along the wall, the huge black grate, the padded leather chairs were as spotless and impersonal. All the fears that had risen in her as a child when she had sat there waiting for her first meeting with Mother St Sophie rose in her now. She heard herself cry out, as then she had done, 'This is a prison. I'm frightened,' because she had suspected that her mother had betrayed her, that it was an institution to which she was being abandoned as a wayward and ungovernable child.

From the walls well-remembered portraits of Pius IX, St Augustine, Henry V, the founder, stared down at her but there was also a picture she did not recall. It was a copy of a section of a mural she had seen on a visit to the Panthéon. It depicted Joan of Arc at the stake. Surely it had not been there in her childhood. Then from a door opposite a short plump nun entered. Again it seemed as if the past was being relived for had not, on that first occasion, a short, round little woman entered the waiting-room? She had raised her face to Sarah, the sweetest, merriest face imaginable : large blue eyes, a turned-up nose, a laughing mouth, beautiful strong white teeth, a face of such humanity and kindness that Sarah had hugged her in relief. This simply could not be Mother St Sophie now. She had died seven years ago. The resemblance was uncanny.

The new Superior of the Grand-Champ Convent set her at ease. Sarah explained why she had come. It was a sentimental journey, she said, but one she hoped would confirm her resolve to start a new life in a different setting. The Mother Superior took her on a tour of the house and grounds which had altered little over the years – the white dormitories, the plain tables in the refectory, the enormous triptych of the Holy Family above the door to the garden, and the grounds themselves with their vegetable plots and hard uncomfortable benches beside the gravel paths. A strange feeling of disembodiment overtook her. It was as though she were outside herself detachedly observing this visit as once, as a child, she had watched the ageing Rachel tour these gardens, short of breath and feeble. She had been told later by the thin-lipped nun who taught them botany that Rachel had lived a life of evil intemperance and was being punished for it now. Was there a child among the hundreds of hidden faces watching her now to be told that evening that their visitor was Sarah Bernhardt and that her name was bathed in shame?

Before she left they returned to the waiting-room. She asked about the picture of Joan of Arc which she could not recall as having hung there. The Mother Superior confirmed this, explaining that it had been in another part of the convent for many years. Mother St Sophie had ordered its transfer to the waiting-room the day before she died. Again Sarah's head was full of voices. She lingered a while before the picture, but when she said farewell to the Mother Superior it was with a sense of emptiness and disappointment. For it seemed that no message had awaited her after all.

On the train back to Paris she was reflective but serene. Perhaps the convent's gift to her was a quiet mind, the acceptance of her position. In the morning she would arrange for the sale of her house.

As the train rattled across Paris she was interested to see a theatre that once she had played in was no longer being used. The showman in her was always offended by a playhouse gone 'dark', to use the profession's term, for a lifeless stage was like consecrated land weed-infested. Places of worship and entertainment were equally sacrosanct. Such a sight spurred an urge to reclaim it, for she had desired her own theatre. But that was not feasible now. Before the débâcle it had seemed possible. What was the point of dreaming? Yet for the rest of the journey the vision persisted: 'The Sarah Bernhardt Theatre presents . . .' Presents what? And who would come to see her?

At home she found Madame Guérard reading. It was already twilight and she told her not to strain her eyes.

Mam'selle put down her book.

'What are you reading?' she asked.

'One of Maurice's school history books, the trial of Joan of Arc,' Madame Guérard answered.

Sarah lit the gas jets. 'Read me some,' she said.

Mam'selle read the Executioner's account: '"The day when Joan was burned the wood was got ready to burn her before the sermon was finished or the sentence had been pronounced. And no sooner the sentence uttered by the bishop, without any delay she was taken to the fire, and I did not see that there was any sentence pronounced by the lay judge. And in the fire she cried more than six times 'Jesus', and above all with her last breath she cried in a loud voice 'Jesus!' so that all present could hear her. Almost all wept with pity, and I have heard say that the ashes, after her burning, were gathered up and cast into the Seine."'

'Why did you choose that particular book?' Sarah asked.

'Because she has become the spirit of our lost provinces,' Madame Guérard replied. 'Joan was a Lorrainer and is at last coming into her own. She has had to wait four and a half centuries. It is high time someone revived Jules Barbier's play.'

To a person less sensitive to signs and portents the day's omens would have held some significance. To Sarah they seemed like an undeniable call. The more she thought of Joan, the more her timeliness became more apparent, parallels multiplied. Joan was a simple patriot from Lorraine. She saved the city of Orleans, which commanded the principal bridge over the Loire. It was the artery through which the English in the fifteenth century planned to extend their invasion of France and hunt down the Dauphin Charles. Orleans was the indispensable crossing place, its capture essential. So the English put it to siege and reduced it to starvation. But just as it was seeking surrender the news broke like thunder – Orleans had been relieved! The English had raised the siege in the face of 'the Maid bearing a banner'.

All this had happened in a France divided, torn apart from within as well as by the enemy, and anyone who had lived through 1870 and its aftermath could see similarities. Since then Frenchmen had 'stared hypnotized by the gap in the Vosges' at the French city of Strasbourg and the provinces of Alsace and Lorraine now being forcibly Germanized. In the story of Joan was a focus for the pride and ambition of a France still bruised and suffering from her humiliating defeat, aware that there would never be lasting peace in Europe until the lost provinces had been regained.

Already in the 1880s there had begun a campaign involving Church and State, carefully observed by the public and debated in the Press, to make Joan's day of triumph over the English a national holiday. In time she would become so potent a symbol of national fervour that many would pray for her reincarnation for the purpose of chasing the Germans from the captured areas. What a character! She was the stuff of dreams and yearnings. In this rejected, spurned young woman she saw a vehicle for her own rehabilitation, for her own triumphant return!

By morning she was ready to explain to Mam'selle what she had in mind. If the unused theatre she had seen were available she intended to lease and renovate it. Then she would form a company of her own and open with Barbier's *Joan of Arc*. To finance the venture she would use her house as collateral.

But as she waited for Mam'selle to come to her bedroom with the early-morning tray and the newspapers, as was her custom again now that Damala had gone, she wondered if she had the heart to tell her old friend. It was a terrible gamble. Had she the right to take it? Did she not owe to Mam'selle the retreat they had talked about, a life of comparative ease, an end to the crises of the theatre? For if she failed there would be nothing, not even a home for Maurice or any of them. Surely it was immoral to put her ego above the needs of others yet again. Damala was right when he told her that glitter and applause had blinded her to what life was really about. By the time she heard Mam'selle approaching she had decided to put aside the wild scheme.

Mam'selle placed the tray and the newspapers on her bedside table. She poured the hot chocolate. The quiet familiarity of it all stirred memories.

'Do you remember the morning of my first audition?' she asked. 'You were pouring the chocolate when I asked you to hear my lines.'

'"Once upon a time there were two pigeons, who loved each other deeply, as brothers do."' Mam'selle began the fable so firmly imprinted on both their minds. 'Can you remember the next line?' she asked Sarah.

'"But one of them grew tired of the familiar hills and valleys of their country and yearned to . . ."' Sarah stopped reciting. She was in tears.

Mam'selle sat on the bed beside her and for several minutes they were silent. She took her hand. 'There's only one cure for you,' she said. 'I simply cannot see you as a dressmaker and after all these years I really couldn't face it myself. I'd miss the theatre as much as you would. If you've been offered something then take it. Last night there was a suggestion of the old fire. Tell me, Sarah. Tell me what we're going to do.'

Together they talked about her plan. They drank the chocolate and had no time to open a newspaper.

If they had done so they might have read a small item in the *Figaro.* It reported the success achieved in one year by Marie Colombier's *The Memoirs of Sarah Barnum.* It had sold a million copies. As the newspaper pointed out, it had led to the retirement of Sarah Bernhardt – 'the former actress'.

CHAPTER 19

The once elegant theatre on the Place du Châtelet was more dilapidated than expected but she obtained a lease on it and began its restoration. Her bank valued her house at a very considerable sum but every penny was to be needed to meet the huge costs involved. It was mortgaged lock, stock and barrel, for she had to pay for what amounted to the rebuilding of the theatre's interior as well as its external repairs. Then she had to pay a staff and hire a company of actors and still have funds enough for promotion and the innumerable running costs. Sarah laboured day and night, getting little sleep, pressing the work forward, encouraging, persuading, arguing, cajoling with Madame Guérard ever in attendance.

A wonderful thing happened. The little people of the theatre, the seamstresses, carpenters, dressers who had heard about her venture came to help, working voluntarily, sometimes coming after a day's work and staying late into the night, and this moved her deeply. That alone would have given her the courage to go on. But Sardou was frankly dubious when she took him to see the theatre. The repairs had been started and as they toured the circle lumps of stucco fell into the stalls. He strongly advised her against the plan but she told him that her course was set. 'Is there another way?' she asked.

Within three months the huge theatre was transformed and with many innovations. There was electric lighting instead of gas in the auditorium as well as for stage effects. The upholstery and panelling were in contrasting yellow and white instead of the traditional red plush and gilt. The foyer, in the same colour scheme, was adorned with Bernhardt memorabilia such as the Clairin portrait, a bronze bust of her, the Mucha posters and old billboards in frames. Above the entrance to the theatre in *art nouveau* filigree were huge iron letters proclaiming The Sarah Bernhardt Theatre and below that almost as prominent: 'The Sarah Bernhardt Company presents Jules Barbier's *Joan of Arc.*' It was a bold challenge, for her name still gave offence.

It was in fact asking for trouble. Already letters had arrived, invariably anonymous, warning her not to set foot on a Paris stage. Their tone was not just hostile, it was sometimes very sick. The well-known fact that she was part-Jewish influenced some of these shady correspondents to resort to anti-Semitic obscenities and some even threatened violence. The most frightening of all suggested that her son could be victimized. She hadn't thought it possible that spite of this kind existed – even at the lunatic fringe – and these letters compounded her worries. But she continued the rehearsals and advertised her impending return.

A few hours before the first-night opening, when she was at the theatre checking costumes and scenery, she was informed that there was a young woman at the stage-door asking for her. She was wary and asked that the caller be brought to the auditorium so that she would not be alone when they met. But the harmlessness of her visitor was at once apparent, a slim, pretty, but obviously distressed girl of about eighteen.

'Please, Madame Bernhardt, you must come with me,' she said. 'I think Monsieur Damala is dying.'

As the carriage took them along the Rue Tronchet, passed the Madeleine and into the Rue Royale, the girl related how she had met Damala. He had been in Algeria for several months, it seemed, and on his return had arrived at her mother's house asking for a room. On realizing how ill he was they had befriended him. That afternoon they had found him in a condition of collapse and able only to speak her name. Her mother had been an admirer of Sarah's and knew where she could be found, but feared it might already be too late. Sarah felt an immense tenderness towards the simple-hearted girl.

The carriage drew up outside a humble apartment house. They climbed the worn stone steps to the third floor and found him in a room littered with bottles and strewn with clothes and crumpled newspapers. It smelled heavily of brandy. There was evidence of cocaine and morphia and on the filthy floor was a broken hypodermic syringe. Damala lay bare-chested on a narrow bed. On his body the needle marks had festered and he was flabbily fat. Yet his eyes still shone, his face had its familiar cynical smile. The girl left them together.

'It's Sarah, my love,' she said. He turned his face away and she said again, 'My love.'

'My love?' He murmured something else but it was hardly audible. She was too distraught for tears. How could she comfort him?

'I never wanted to quarrel . . .' she began.

He appeared to rally. 'I assure you, it isn't difficult to die.' It was a line from *Camille* written in her memory like music. She put a hand to his head.

'You spoke it . . . played it very well,' she said. His face was full of sorrow and yearning and perplexity. 'When you are better we'll work again together. I have my own theatre now. Tonight, Aristide . . .' But she knew that he was already dead.

For some time she remained motionless at the bedside, introspective, heavy with failure. That her love for Damala was ill-starred she had really known from their first meeting. She could have drawn back from it many times. After the bitter quarrels its hopelessness had been clear to both of them. Yet they had continued as if gripped in the dark purpose of using his weakness to keep her strong.

It had been simple and reassuring for people to conclude

that he was a wastrel using and degrading her, but the truth was known only to herself. She had seen his good intentions go unfulfilled, lived through moments of uncomplicated familiarity with him, known that he had often considered reclaiming himself but had neglected to do so not merely out of waywardness or folly or disregard for her but out of self-contempt. Damala, she believed, had been someone so aware of his own inadequacy, so conscious of his fatal flaw that he hid it in arrogance. It was his only façade.

He had found in her ambition, her self-willed sense of destiny, her claim to be unconventional, her very success an even tougher arrogance, more realistically based, more resilient and far more profound than the attempt he made at it. Their wills clashed at every climax. But she was convinced, and always would be, that but for his addiction he would have been as proud, possessive and vital as herself, and as capable of staying young. In her he had met his destiny. He had fulfilled it by revealing to her the responsibility of her gift and the illusory nature of romantic passion – or so she would rationalize.

How then could she honour him? His body, she decided, would be returned to Greece. On his tomb would be placed the bust she had made of him. And to the end of her life she would describe herself, except professionally, as Madame Sarah Bernhardt Damala.

On her return to the theatre she noticed that a crowd had gathered around the marquee. Tickets must be selling well. But had they come to jeer? Mam'selle confirmed her fears.

'The theatre will be packed,' she said, 'but it will be a mob, not an audience. I've been watching the foyer. Troublemakers are buying tickets. You must not go on, Sarah. It could be dangerous.' But Mam'selle knew she would not heed.

She began putting on her make-up, something she always

did herself. The application of the greasepaints, rouges and powders was a ritual. She would never trust it to anyone else. Then her hairdresser came in to clip, comb, press and plait the rebellious hair. In time it had taken on the clean-cut boyish style of Joan. Then her dresser helped her into the doublet and hose of the Maid. In time the marvellous transformation was complete – a woman of thirty-five had become the nineteen-year-old Joan of Lorraine. But Sarah was doubting whether she had the courage to go on. Mam'selle's concern didn't help. 'Please, I beg of you, cancel the performance. It isn't worth it, Sarah.'

She thought of Damala's dying, and it strengthened her resolve not to retreat now.

'Some of them have brought stones to throw.'

'I want you to go home,' she said quietly but firmly to Mam'selle. The old lady hesitated, kissed her and then silently left the room.

The call-boy came to announce that it was time. As she walked to the wings someone called to her: 'Please don't go on.' It might have been Sardou. But her mind was listening to the Dauphin.

'You say they call her the Maid?' came the voice from the stage.

'Yes, sire,' replied a courtier.

'Do you think I should see her?' asked the Dauphin.

'The men think highly of her,' the courtier replied.

Then a ribald voice from the audience shouted, 'We think she's a whore.' The laughter that followed was mingled with mock applause. It was the most chilling sound she had ever heard.

'Well, then, send her in,' said the Dauphin.

Sarah hesitated. The hoots and catcalls grew more boisterous.

The Dauphin struggled on: 'I will disguise myself among you and if she can choose which of us is the true ruler of France I shall hear what she has to say.' He hid among his courtiers. 'Send her in.'

'Send her in, send her in,' echoed the crowd and it became a chant to the rhythm of stamping feet. 'Send her in, send her in, send her in.'

'In the name of God don't go on.' Sardou was standing beside her, but she hardly noticed him.

'Where's Joan?' asked a courtier.

'Where's Sarah?' demanded a voice from the audience. 'Where's that Jewish slut who made a whore of herself in England?'

'Madame Bernhardt, let me lower the curtain,' pleaded the stage-manager, but she motioned him aside. She stepped on to the stage and there was a furore of hisses and catcalls. The splash of rotten vegetables hit the boards.

'Are you the maid called Joan of Lorraine?' asked a courtier. He could barely be heard above the din.

'I am, sire,' she replied. She had said it too faintly for she felt quelled by the savagery. 'I am,' she said more firmly.

'Speak up, Joan. We can't hear you.' A hoodlum banged on a metal pail. 'Go back to the English!'

'If you are sent from God, as you say you are,' the courtier persisted, but he was fighting a losing battle, 'you can certainly divine the blood royal.'

'That's what she did in London,' someone shouted from the pit. 'She slept with the Prince of Wales.'

'But what if she's sent from the Devil?' asked the second courtier.

'Send her back to him – that's all she's fit for.'

It was the point of decision – should she give up or continue to try? She recognized the Dauphin. 'God give you life, gentle king.'

'I am not the King, Joan. There is the King,' said the Dauphin, pointing to one of his courtiers.

'By God, gentle prince, it is you and none other.'

Smiling, the Dauphin realized Joan's powers. 'So you are the Maid called Joan.'

'I am, sire,' said Sarah. A stone hit the stage. Then a volley – stones, fruit, shoes, bags of flour – and a fire-cracker exploded in the stalls. Her actors were terrified, but she stood firm and urged them to continue.

'Why have you come?' asked the Dauphin.

'I've been sent to save France,' she replied. A bit of a broken cup hit her cheek.

It was the final insult. Furious, shaking, she walked directly down stage. There was no retreating now. A mob had no sanctity. To bow to it was a betrayal. So she faced up to them squarely with a hostility more daunting than their own.

'*I have been sent by God to you – to save the Kingdom*,' she proclaimed. The voice was awesome. It had its cathedral quality again, profound and terrible with conviction. 'It is time for us to arise . . .'

'And go home,' interrupted a hoodlum but without authority. The audience was now listening to her.

'It is time for us to bring our nation victory. Under my banner. With God and the Maid beside you *France shall be saved*.'

Each word was a missile more indicting than anything they had thrown. 'God has sent me to you to lead you to Rheims and there see you crowned. Will you give me an army?'

The Dauphin plucked up courage. 'What are the reasons for your faith? Tell us.'

'It is God's pleasure, sire . . .'

They were enthralled. The magic was working. She had them in her power. As the play proceeded backstage faces looked on in wonder. Eventually she reached the trial scene.

'You have tried me and found me guilty. You, in your

infinite wisdom, have sentenced me to burn at the stake. You say I am an heretic, a non-believer. You say I have done things no woman should do. That is true . . .'

It was her own confession too and the audience accepted it as such. '. . . but I am afraid no longer, not of you, not of the fire.'

Act followed act and the thrall in which she held them deepened until at the scene of the burning their respect was total. She was able to make her final speeches against a silence so profound that the significance of that terrible ceremony united them in an infinite dream, spun from their tears and her folly. She had won.

'Dear God, must it be by burning? Must this flesh be consumed in flames? Must this body be burned to ashes? Scattered to the winds? Oh, dear God, spare me!'

At the stake she beheld a vision, a face unknown, a composite – was it Damala's, Judith's, Henri's? A thousand faces seemed to mingle. 'I can see him! God the father! Stretching out his hand to me among the flames! Dear God, how can you give me gifts beyond all others, show me divine secrets, and then leave me to the mob? . . .

'Why have you put me here to suffer for their pleasure? Why have you sent me into this life to be torn away from it in suffering and in pain? . . .

'Father, will I die in vain and never be remembered? Will those who love me banish me from memory? And shall it be as though I never lived? Dear God, speak!'

Every eye sought Sarah's. Would there be an answer? And with an art that disguises all pretence to it she crossed herself and almost imperceptibly smiled. She had seen her vision.

'I come, precious Lord, to the comfort of your bosom. I come gladly to eternal life. Burn me. Destroy my body, yet I shall live for ever. I see you, dear Father, and I come to you within the flames.'

As the flames shot up from the base of the stake the

audience heard a scream so horrible that the descending curtain was a shield, their only defence against what was no longer bearable. It rose and they were silent. Then suddenly, they were on their feet to cheer. The people had reclaimed their Sarah – and Paris was hers again.

POSTSCRIPT: THE VINTAGE YEARS

Sarah lived on for almost half a century during which she worked incessantly, touring Europe, playing frequently in England, crossing the Atlantic several times to tour the American continent, north to south, east to west, in her special train, playing to city audiences in the grandest of theatres and to more lowly ones in mission halls.

Like every diva she was loath to say goodbye and so there were Farewell Tours followed by Second Farewell Tours and, amazingly, Third Farewell Tours – never a final tour.

A World Tour lasted two whole years and took her to 80 American and Canadian cities, to Australia and New Zealand, to Hawaii, to Brazil and Argentine, to England, Portugal, Belgium, Holland, Hungary, Russia, Austria, Turkey, Greece, Egypt, Italy, Sicily and Switzerland.

She seems to have been driven all her life by quite superhuman energies for she was always restless, always seeking 'another atmosphere, a vaster space, other skies'. She must have been very difficult to live with and not surprisingly did not marry again, though it is evident that she had many loves. When Madame Guérard died, wizened and absent-minded but faithful to the end, she had Maurice's family to give her companionship and in the brief interludes between her tours she delighted in the role of grandmother. She never denied her age, only defied it on stage.

The roles she played were legion – a mixture of the ephemeral and the classic, the lightweight and profound. And there were what Sir John Gielgud has called 'her strange, transvestite excursions' – Hamlet ('a very great lady indeed,' commented Sir Max Beerbohm), Lorenzaccio, Pelleas, and Napoleon's youthful son (in *L'Aiglon*) whom she played at the age of fifty-five.

Gielgud, incidentally, saw her when he was thirteen at the London Coliseum and was 'spellbound' even though by then she had only one leg, the other having been amputated above the knee after she had endured years of pain. After the operation she usually appeared on stage seated or at ease on a chaise-longue draped in a coverlet. But still she went on touring and in the First World War was carried by car and chair to the Western Front to entertain the troops.

Obviously she was the first international star to realize the power of publicity. At that time of the growth of the mass-circulation newspapers there were always Press conferences when she arrived at a city or town, and she invariably made the headlines with her outspokenness and eccentricities. She was never afraid to speak her mind, a thinking woman with views on all the major political and social questions of her day. She was pro-Dreyfus during that great French national scandal. She was against capital punishment. She was a prophet of women's liberation though she would never have liked that label, for she was always a liberated spirit herself.

In her seventies, her face masked by rouge and mascara, an enchantress in leopard skins, she relished the new hunting ground of the 1920s, finding much to her taste for she had helped to set the scene. She had also become fascinated by the movies.

This woman, ever young, suspected that in the infant kinescope lay some hope of permanence, so she made *Hamlet* (a pioneer of pioneer film-making for it was made in 1890 and had sound synchronized to film) and, silently, *Queen Elizabeth* and various single-reelers which now repose in the archives of museums in Paris, London and New York.

There are some nineteen posthumous biographies of which Cornelia Otis Skinner's comes closest to revealing the living quality behind the legend. Her own memoirs are rambling but they echo with her magnanimity and at moments reveal her selfishness. From this conglomerate of writings one gets a vision of a star more durable than those who were later able to bequeath their fast-dating movies to the television screen. Those who died young, like Valentino, James Dean or Marilyn Monroe, acted out small tragedies at once fascinating and deplorable, but Bernhardt played out her life until she was nearly eighty and died greatly honoured, a Chevalier of the Legion of Honour, in 1923. That was the difference. She managed to endure.

I was in a backwater of Mexico when I received a letter from Helen M. Strauss saying that she was going to produce *Sarah* with Glenda Jackson in the title role. I had been there for so long that even the godly sight of the sunsets over the Sea of Cortes had begun to pall, working on a film of wild extravagance and dubious verisimilitude. But Sarah would have loved the titanic, circus-like scale of the film location, the crowds of heterogeneous extras, the two hundred technicians, the multi-million-dollar budget and the retinue of courtiers surrounding the stars.

As it happened I had been reading a history of the movies in which it was reported that on being invited to film *Camille* at the age of sixty-five (one hand-cranked camera, a technical crew of three) she had jumped at the chance, declaring, 'This is my one chance of immortality.' What a truly touching fear, I thought, was revealed in that remark.

Did she then wonder if all her 'live' performances would become whispers and disappear without trace into the thin air, that all the years of stardom would prove translucent, that the light when it failed would go out for ever? She need not have worried. She would be remembered in the realm of legend. She had created her own.

She had once told the Duchess of Teck, mother of Queen

Mary, George V's consort, 'I will die on the stage. It is my battleground.' She very nearly did. While filming for the flickering silent screen one of her pastiche pieces, *The Fortune Teller*, she picked up the ace of spades and collapsed, dramatic to the end. A few days later she died.

She was laid to rest in a simple mausoleum in the Cemetery of Père Lachaise which bears the epitaph : 'Here lies Bernhardt – who will survive.'

That same year she had given an interview to the London *Daily Telegraph* : 'You ask me my theory of life. It is represented in one word, *will* . . . Life is short, even for those of us who live a long time, and we must live for the few who know and appreciate us, who judge and absolve us, and for whom we have the same affection and indulgence. We ought to hate very rarely, as it is too fatiguing, remain indifferent a great deal, forgive often, and never forget.'

As Lytton Strachey said the year she died : 'There was more than gold. There was thunder and lightning. There was heaven and hell.'

And she came to be called – Divine.

Winston Graham

'One of the best half-dozen novelists in this country.' *Books and Bookmen*. 'Winston Graham excels in making his characters come vividly alive.' *Daily Mirror*. 'A born novelist.' *Sunday Times*

His immensely popular suspense novels include:

Take My Life
The Sleeping Partner
Fortune is a Woman
Angell, Pearl and Little God

Winston Graham has also written The Poldark Saga, his famous story of eighteenth-century Cornwall:

Ross Poldark
Demelza
Jeremy Poldark
Warleggan
The Black Moon

And three historical novels:

The Grove of Eagles
The Forgotten Story
Cordelia

Howard Spring

In 1938 his most famous book, *My Son, My Son*, was published; it was a world-wide success. Since then all his books, without exception, have been best-sellers and have earned Howard Spring a high reputation as an author of universal appeal.

'Howard Spring is a novelist of solid and considerable talent, whose ability to tell a story, sense of character, craftmanship and industry should put hollower and more pretentious novelists to shame.' *Spectator*

'He is not afraid of stark drama, and he writes with real feeling.' *Sunday Times*

Shabby Tiger

I Met a Lady

A Sunset Touch

Winds of the Day

These Lovers Fled Away

Fontana Books

Fontana Books

Fontana is a leading paperback publisher of fiction and non-fiction, with authors ranging from Alistair MacLean, Agatha Christie and Desmond Bagley to Solzhenitsyn and Pasternak, from Gerald Durrell and Joy Adamson to the famous Modern Masters series.

In addition to a wide-ranging collection of internationally popular writers of fiction, Fontana also has an outstanding reputation for history, natural history, military history, psychology, psychiatry, politics, economics, religion and the social sciences.

All Fontana books are available at your bookshop or newsagent; or can be ordered direct. Just fill in the form and list the titles you want.

FONTANA BOOKS, Cash Sales Department, G.P.O. Box 29, Douglas, Isle of Man, British Isles. Please send purchase price, plus 8p per book. Customers outside the U.K. send purchase price, plus 10p per book. Cheque, postal or money order. No currency.

NAME (Block letters)

ADDRESS

While every effort is made to keep prices low, it is sometimes necessary to increase prices on short notice. Fontana Books reserve the right to show new retail prices on covers which may differ from those previously advertised in the text or elsewhere.